ALSO BY CAMBRIA WILLIAMS

THE UNSUNG AND THE WOLF DUOLOGY

The Befallen

Keeper of the Word

A HERO'S TITLE

A CAPELLA REALM NOVELLA

CAMBRIA WILLIAMS

PURPLE GATE PRESS
MMXXIV

A HERO'S TITLE

Cover Art and Design by Natalie Brianne
nataliebrianne.com

Map by Mayank Sharma
dzign.in

Purple Gate Press

PURPLE GATE
PRESS

The Library of Congress Cataloging-in-Publication Data is available upon request.

ISBN 979-8-9920670-0-2 (Paperback)

ISBN 979-8-9920670-1-9 (ebook)

In loving memory of my sweet Belle.
And for all the animal companions who are our friends.

DEOGOL

THE BLOCK

MONAS TERRITORY

THE NEREZZA

ROCK - AND - TREE

THE BOG

BRANWELL

SLOUGH GROTH

CHAPTER
1

The long road had no end. At least, that was how it seemed to Alvie. He had already spent more than a week traveling on the weathered-down route from Dara Keep to Kage Duna. Although he'd been enthralled at the beginning of the journey, the sense of adventure clinging to the chill of the Hunger Moon air, he had long since lost his enthusiasm. He was sore, travel-weary, and worst of all, bored.

He rode Kenn, a tall, grey stallion, who had belonged to his best friend, Sloane. Well, in truth, Kenn belonged to the Cibil of the Nay Moon, which was why Alvie was trekking all the way to Kage Duna. That was a long story, and although Alvie loved long stories, there was no one to tell it to just now so he simply plodded along, whistling or singing random verses of his favorite folk songs like "The Bard Cries Weasel" and "Shalalan," watching his cold breath come out in puffs. Every so often, Kenn would be forced to jerk to a halt by the mule being led behind them. Alvie tugged at the mule's rope, speaking to the beast like he was a bothersome bar mate who'd stumbled his way into Alvie's party.

"Come on now, you ol' goat."

In return, the mule twitched his ears, snorting and turning its head to gaze at the frosted plains along the horizon.

"It ain't time to eat. Come on now."

Kenn neighed, as if berating the mule, and the three trotted along once more.

Alvie gave the mule a backward glance. A mule. A knight of the Order of Siria should have a horse! But the Order knights of Dara Keep were, themselves, worse for the wear, and unsurprisingly, had no horse to spare for Alvie's return journey. Alvie couldn't blame them. After all, the Order *had* been cut in half after the Battle for the Unsung two moons ago. Yet he was, too, aware that although Ghlee, the new commander of the Order of Siria, more than accepted Alvie—welcomed him and considered him his brother now—a few of the knights did not give him the same endorsement.

Alvie rolled his eyes in annoyance.

This was not new. The coarse attitudes of others landed on Alvie like unwelcome flies on a sweaty day. Alvie wasn't stupid. He was fully aware his appearance lacked the usual qualities of a knight: he was shorter than most men and built like the peg leg that'd replaced his right leg below the kneecap decades ago after a bout of the Cors fever. He'd spent much of his life as a pauper or as a short-term laborer working for mere coppers. He wasn't stupid.

But he'd had twenty-two years of brushing off others' discouragement. The silly, small opinions of others would never be Alvie's concern.

And now, Alvie had great stories to tell! *Real* stories. Stories of how he'd helped–nay, assisted? Nay. Aided! Aye, Alvie had aided the Unsung. That had a ring to it. He'd been *in* the battle. Had swung his mighty starstone club to defeat many men. Had defended Sloane from a murderous Ravyn! Had witnessed the destruction of the Befallen, a dark curse that had slain thousands in the five years it had terrorized their island kingdom of Deogol. And Alvie had been there upon its defeat. Such a story Alvie had never told or heard in his life. And 'twas his story now. Alvie's chest swelled with pride for a moment before it sank again thinking of his friend. Sloane the Unsung.

He knew she would be proud of him. She would never ask him to deny his own part of what had happened that day. But Alvie had not counted many people in his life as friends. True friends. A true friend was as rare as finding a singular star. But Sloane had been his true friend. And he missed her.

At least he had the Order of Siria now. The others may be slow to accept Alvie, but they'd come around. People usually did. This was an experience as ordinary to Alvie's life as his wanderings. And Alvie was a part of something now. He smiled, contemplating the great adventures that were in store. And when he returned to Dara Keep, he would have somewhere to call home.

EVENTUALLY THE ROAD STRETCHED NORTH OF AYLA, a place that for Alvie had plenty of stories of its own, and turned dense with trees. Although Alvie preferred the open road—it was a great deal easier to mark approaching travelers —the shelter of the trees insulated the road somewhat from the winter air. Alvie had no love for being cold. He knew it sounded mad to those with all their limbs, but in cold weather, a tingling would run up and down the ghost of his right leg, causing a phantom pain that should not exist. He'd taken to never commenting on this to others, but fact o'matter was, warm was better.

They rested for the night, and Alvie found another welcome benefit of being off the open road: he did not have to trudge through deep snow. He was nimble to be sure, much more so than first impressions would warrant, but he didn't mind having an easier time grooming and bedding Kenn and the mule for the night. And tonight would be the first night in four evenings he'd have a fire since the wood wasn't damp.

Alvie struck the flint against the fire steel, welcoming the cheery glow of warmth as the evening's company.

If Alvie found himself bored during the slow days of travel, they were nothing compared to the loneliness of night. Stories were difficult to tell when alone. Despite that, Alvie would still enfold his cloak around himself and concoct new tales in his mind. He would have to run into an inn eventually or at least a cottage. Anyone.

The mule snorted nearby.

"I s'pose I could tell you a tale. You wanna hear about the time I won a jig contest in Vithal?"

The mule turned away. Apparently not.

With naught else to do, and not being so reckless that he dared sing, Alvie rummaged through his saddle bags, ensuring all was in order. As he'd performed the same activity yesternight, he found everything was indeed still in order.

He withdrew his new moon cuff, a leather wristlet meant for prayer to the goddesses of the full moon. He didn't consider himself superstitious but did not place it on his wrist. Instead, he examined the stamped imprints of the different moon symbols, quizzing himself on the twelve goddesses. Technically, there were thirteen, but few had the Azure Moon symbol on their moon cuff. In no time, Alvie grew bored, as he had the night before, and placed it back in the saddle bag.

A scurry from the nearby underbrush caught Alvie's attention. He held the starstone club at the ready.

"Oi! Someone there?" Alvie said into the night, the fire's light flickering off the trunks and surrounding bushes.

A second sound of scuttling quickened his heartbeat. He tightened his grip on the club.

"Hallo?"

The underbrush shook. Alvie gave an involuntary yelp and lifted the club higher above his head, then he lowered it. The glow from the fire bounced on a particular bush as it swayed.

His brows drew together. "Hallo?"

The bustling continued. Something was caught in that bush.

Carefully, Alvie approached, noting the many thorns protruding from its thin branches. Stars, how would he part the branches enough to see with all those tiny thorns?

Using his club, Alvie separated the top branches as much as they would give. Even with the firelight, it was difficult to peer down to the bottom.

The scuttering intensified. Whatever was in the bush fought with everything it had to free itself.

"Hold still," Alvie said, as if this small creature would cease its flailing. At least it couldn't be a shadow cat. Alvie had had enough of those to last a lifetime.

Alvie dug the club in deeper to glimpse whatever it was that made this bush shudder like the prey of a banshee. Finally, Alvie caught a brief look at the creature. A small animal with an extraordinarily bushy tail.

His breath hitched.

"Nah," Alvie whispered to himself. "It can't be." He wouldn't let himself say it. He would not name the animal he felt certain was ensnared here.

The tail jerked as the animal thrashed around. 'Twas clear that 'twas its tail that was caught. Alvie squinted through the dim light to try and determine where the tail was trapped. With one hand still on the club to part the thorny branches, Alvie reached for where he suspected he might free the tail.

The bush swayed and he snapped back his arm. His hand bled from a scratch made from tiny claws.

"I'm tryin' to help you!"

The thrashing did not cease. If anything, Alvie's attempt to help had provoked it to desperation.

Alvie examined his hand as he pondered what to try next. Without help, there would be no way to free this creature without wounds, whether from the thorns or its claws or both.

"Fact o'matter is, ye got to hold still or I'm not gonna be able to help you."

The small creature paused, giving Alvie a moment to gaze down at it.

He sucked in his breath. It couldn't be. But it had to be.

What else could it be?

It thrashed about again, revealing no additional details about itself. But it had to be, nothing else fit the description. About the size of a tom cat, the creature had ears like a lop-eared rabbit. But the bushy tail that was the length of its body meant it was definitely *not* a rabbit. Not to mention Alvie had managed to touch its fur. Soft. Softer than anything he had ever felt. To Alvie's mind, all evidence made clear what this creature was.

Here was a hoshefer.

The rarest of all creatures on the continent of Tasia. Rarer than even the dragons in Vathnava. Whether their rarity was due to being hunted down before it had been outlawed in all realms or that they were simply that scarce, Alvie didn't know, but what he did know was that he was gawking at one right now.

"Holy stars," Alvie said to the thrashing hoshefer.

Cuts and scrapes be damned, Alvie just had to help this little hoshefer. He yearned for some gloves before reaching his hand into the snarling branches once more. Immediately, the hoshefer's claws pierced his hand. He yelped at the knife-like tears along his skin, but blindly searched his hand along the frantically whipping tail until he located the thorn that bit into it.

The sounds Alvie made weren't knight-like, but even the bravest knight he knew, Sir Tolvar, the Wolf, would be shouting. Alvie was certain.

As carefully as he could, Alvie untangled the thorn from the long hairs in the hoshefer's tail.

The moment it broke free, the hoshefer scampered out of the bush and sprinted into the night. Alvie withdrew his cut-up hand from the bush, bringing his bleeding thumb to his mouth.

He groaned. "No need to thank me!"

Sitting next to the campfire, Alvie inspected the hand that had been the hoshefer's target, counting the seventeen cuts it had left. His other hand had a large scrape, too, from jerking it out of the bush. A thorn still hung from it. Alvie pinched it between his fingers and yanked it out.

He thanked his lucky stars he had a salve in his saddle bag. Alvie rubbed it on his hands before bandaging the more injured of the two in a strip of cloth he kept with the salve.

Despite his throbbing hands, Alvie smiled, his silver tooth glinting in the firelight. A *real* hoshefer. One more story to add to his collection.

CHAPTER
2

Alvie knew he must be in Kage Duna when the evergreen and pine-oak trees they'd been passing transformed into small quag trees slumping in grey swamps. Other enormous trees, covered in vines and moss, towered over everything, enclosing the place in a pale, stagnant gloom.

"Right cheery here. Just like I remember," Alvie said, wrapping his cloak around himself as if it might protect any last bit of high spirits he *did* have. The musty odor didn't help matters. Alvie crinkled his nose.

His hand still throbbed, but a few days had gone by, and Alvie wasn't one to dwell on injuries.

Kenn's ears perked this way and that.

He knows he's nearly home, Alvie decided.

Here in Kage Duna, 'twas difficult to decipher the moon's phase, but before he'd entered, the half-moon had hung in the sky. Judging how long he'd been traveling since then, Alvie assumed it was close to the Nay Moon, the one night between moon cycles in which there was no moon at all. The night when one could seek the Cibil of the Nay Moon, an elusive and ancient oracle.

Sloane had met the Cibil of the Nay Moon, which, even to Alvie's grand storytelling mind, was quite a feat. Because the Cibil of the Nay Moon, if he was the same man from the tales upon tales upon tales, had to be over one hundred years old. Alvie believed that Sloane had met the Cibil, of course he did—the Cibil had been key to her quest—but a hundred-year-old man lurking about in a desolate swamp was quite the story to swallow. Regardless, Alvie was here on a quest of his own and was anxious to also meet the Cibil.

For more than one reason.

The first was, of course, Alvie's quest to return Kenn to his rightful master. In her story about meeting the Cibil, Sloane had told of her discovery that her horse, Kenn, the only known creature to *ever* survive the Befallen, had belonged, in fact, to the Cibil of the Nay Moon. As Sloane told it, the Cibil rarely left Kage Duna, but in an isolated incident where he had ventured from his home, he'd been robbed of everything including his horse and a magical moonstone called the Edan Stone. It'd been Sloane's belief that Kenn's mysterious resistance to the power of the Befallen was directly connected to the Eden Stone. Quite a story.

But Alvie liked this story and moreover, he liked the idea of reuniting Kenn with the Cibil of the Nay Moon. Returning the stallion to his proper place.

But Alvie didn't lie to himself about the other reason why he sought the Cibil of the Nay Moon. For the legends promised that on the night of a Nay Moon, the Cibil would answer *any* question posed to him. Questions about unknowable secrets. Questions about forgotten pasts. And most intriguingly, questions about the future. Alvie liked this story most of all. Although he did not yet have a specific question in mind to ask the Cibil, he'd not waste that opportunity in a few nights. Nay. One would have to be an utter fool to miss the chance to ask a question to an oracle.

THE MULE WAS STUCK. 'TWAS THE ONLY EXPLANATION. It simply couldn't be too stubborn to move, could it? Alvie tugged and tugged at the rope leading the mule's bridle, but the beast stood stationary, up to its belly in the swamp water. Which meant Alvie was up to his armpits in the frigid, sloggy bog.

"Come on, you ol' goat!" Alvie's hands ached from yanking on the rope.

On the banks, Kenn observed the scene, seeming as irritated as a horse paired with a mule could be. He snorted and waggled his head before ripping some bark off a nearby quag tree to chew.

Alvie released the rope, moved to the edge of the swamp pool, and sat on the bank. "Fine."

Shivering in his wet, slippery clothes, he debated whether or not to ferret out his cloak from Kenn's saddle bag. Deciding that he would rather keep it dry for later when the temperature dropped at night, he rubbed his stump through the wet cloth of his hose. He considered digging out the irritating mud between his stump and the peg leg but concluded that task would be pointless at present. There was still plenty of trudging through the bog to be done. Hoping for some improvement, he adjusted the leather strap through his hose, but that also felt pointless. His leg was already sore from the wet friction the strap had caused above his kneecap.

He gave the mule another glare.

The truth was, it didn't matter if the mule moved or not, Alvie was lost and had no idea which direction to go to find the Cibil. He remembered now that this detail was integral to most stories regarding attempts to find the Cibil. Being lost in Kage Duna seemed to be a necessary step to discovering the man. It made sense. An oracle that could answer anyone's question probably didn't enjoy company.

Alvie's face itched, and before he could stop himself, he brushed his hand across his nose, smearing his face with mud.

"Well, that fits all, don't it."

The mule stared at him, bored.

That evening, after finally moving the mule from the swamp sludge onto as dry a campsite as Alvie could find, he sat hunched against a tree wrapped in his cloak, teeth chattering, staring at his would-be fire. The firewood stood arranged neatly in a triangular formation; the dampness of Kage Duna had prevented him from actually lighting it. He pulled tight the folds of his cloak and shivered against the night's chill. To try to keep his spirits up, he'd allowed himself a bigger-than-usual portion of hardtack for dinner. 'Twas by no means the worst thing Alvie had ever eaten, but the warmth of a fire certainly would have made it taste better.

He was preparing to remove his peg leg and bed down for the night when a noise caught his attention. Alvie flexed his fingers, frowning at his club. He was in no mood for the sound of soft movements making their way toward him. It couldn't be a shadow cat. They stayed clear of such wet terrain as this. It could be a person, but he doubted it. The noise was much too faint to be the tromping of footsteps or even hooves. In fact, it seemed the noise was coming from above, in the trees.

Alvie pushed himself into a standing position, his amputated leg aching where the damp leather strap chafed the skin, and craned his neck to make out what intruded upon his ever-growing grumpy mood. Nothing.

Then as if from nowhere, out of the gloom, something landed on a nearby branch at Alvie's eye level. He startled backward, tripping over the roughness of the ground, and met eyes with the hoshefer.

Unlike Alvie, Kenn, and the mule, it bore not a trace of the sludge of Kage Duna. Its fluffy tail—confirmed to be grey, now that it held still for Alvie to mark it, and dry as could be—curled around the branch as if it helped balance the creature. It tilted its head at Alvie, its tiny nose twitching.

If shadow cats detested a swamp like Kage Duna, surely woodland creatures like hoshefers felt the same. If it'd been following Alvie, it'd taken careful measures to not touch the marshy ground. Alvie pictured this hoshefer covered in the mud and gunk of this place and chuckled.

"You'd probably look like a soaked rat if you were on the ground, I wager."

The hoshefer leaned toward Alvie.

"What you doin' all the way over here, little fella?"

The hoshefer suddenly lifted its neck behind itself as if it had heard a noise. Its floppy ears stood straight. It then faced Alvie and made a chattering sound.

Alvie laughed again. Was it *speaking* to him? "Is that so?"

Behind him, Kenn moved, drawing Alvie's attention, and he glanced back. When he faced forward, the hoshefer had vanished.

He scanned the area, but there was no sign of it amongst the tree branches. "Maybe I dreamed that," he told Kenn.

But just in case, Alvie left a small piece of hardtack on a large branch. He didn't know what hoshefers ate, but there couldn't be much out here to scavenge, and with any luck Alvie would have something else to eat soon with the Cibil.

ALVIE HAD NEVER GIVEN PARTICULAR THOUGHT ABOUT GETTING lost. He'd spent much of his childhood on the streets of Kestriel, the capital city of Deogol, and had made home the winding, twisting blocks of the city. If he happened to turn left instead of right and found himself in an unknown district, he'd simply shrug and discover what this new borough had to offer him. In his experience, it didn't always make a great deal of difference. Once he'd been old enough to seek the world outside Kestriel, Alvie had never lost his curiosity over what one road may offer that other more well-known roads couldn't. If there was a will, there was always an eventual place to sleep and food to fill the belly. Strangers in taverns and pubs were simply friends Alvie hadn't met yet.

But wandering the blank sameness of Kage Duna for four days wasn't like turning an unfamiliar corner in Kestriel. And Alvie missed being dry. Even his cloak was now soggy.

At least the mule had decided to lose his stubbornness. Alvie was sure he was leading them in circles, but the mule seemed content to oblige Alvie's lack of direction. At one point, Alvie hoped that Kenn would sense the direction of his former home and take the lead, but the grey stallion did not prove helpful.

Alvie felt on the brink of giving up and changing tactics from finding the Cibil to simply finding his way *out* of Kage Duna when the hoshefer appeared again. Alvie was a slimy mess by now, but the small creature still appeared fresh, fuzzy, and warm.

It chattered at Alvie again, leaning forward on its branch. This time, however, the hoshefer did not just crane its neck behind itself, but rather paced back and forth on the branch, pausing when its back was turned to Alvie.

"That's a nice lil' dance you got there, but unless you are tryin' to help, I can't watch right now."

The hoshefer stood on its hind legs then, the curl of its tail on the branch securing it effortlessly. It chattered again.

The mule gave an answering bray, and Alvie cocked an eye. "Since when do you talk?"

At that moment, Kenn joined the conversation as well, neighing softly in the direction of the hoshefer. Alvie knew it must be the long, cold days here in Kage Duna, but he was certain Kenn also gave it a small nod.

"Rubbish."

He turned from the hoshefer to gather Kenn's reins and the creature's chatter increased, circling and circling on the branch. The mule brayed.

Alvie sighed. "I know I'm imaginin' all this, but I s'pose I got nothin' else to try."

He tied the mule's rope to Kenn's saddle, took Kenn's reins in his hands, and on foot, led the two toward the hoshefer.

It chattered excitedly and leapt from its branch to a tree behind it. Alvie followed, observing as it performed the act again.

"Blimey. No one is gonna believe this."

CHAPTER 3

Although Alvie had recently become a man of faith, he wasn't new to being a believer in magic. An orphan with a peg leg who'd miraculously survived into his twenties was just the sort of person who knew magic existed and simply took it as it was.

That was how Alvie chose to view the hoshefer. Here was clearly a creature of magic. And so little was actually known about them, so, why not?

He followed the hoshefer, deliberately and with difficulty. 'Twas not easy leading a stallion and a mule through a copse of quag trees and pools of swamp, after all. Not to mention, every now and again his peg leg would become caught in the thick sludge of the bog and he'd have to pause to adjust the strap. Still, he found himself in awe, watching the hoshefer leaping from branch to branch without appearing the least bit unsure or unbalanced. When it had to wait for Alvie to catch up, it stood motionless, regarding him, patient and intent.

When night fell, the hoshefer scampered up a giant tree and disappeared. Alvie attempted to coax it down with hardtack, but when it ignored the offering, he couldn't blame it. In the morning, it appeared on the last branch it'd stood on and led them through the swamps anew.

This continued for another day, and Alvie began to wonder if he was going mad. Following a magical, rare creature through a swampland while leading a curse-proof stallion and a stubborn mule. This was beginning to seem like more a fool's errand than a quest worthy of a bard's song.

"Alvie the fool," he whispered under his breath before shaking his head and chuckling. Abruptly, he lost sight of the hoshefer high in the trees.

"Oi! Where'd you go?" Alvie shouted. He twisted around, frantically searching for any movement and listening for chatter. None came.

After a few moments, Alvie sat on a tree stump. "Bah."

Kenn tugged on his reins, so Alvie let go, assuming the horse was after more bark to snack on. But after a moment's focus, Alvie realized that the terrain had changed.

"Well, I'll be."

Aye, he sat on a *dry* stump. And the ground in front of him was dry as well. And where dozens of quag trees had been his only spectators, in front of him stood giant pine-oaks. Alvie's heartbeat quickened. This had to be it.

Alvie rose from the stump and with timid steps, trod across the dry woodland floor. There wasn't a clear path, nay, but anything different had to be a good sign, and so Alvie made his way through the new scenery, leading Kenn and mule behind him, the hoshefer temporarily forgotten.

In a half-hour's time, Alvie stumbled into a beautiful glade. Immediately, the balminess of the air struck him. Warm. Stars, it was warm. Almost as if Alvie were indoors. He dropped his damp cloak on the ground.

Ground lilies were scattered about the glade, their large white petals appearing almost to glow in the twilight, their fresh scent filling his nostrils.

"Those should not be growin' yet." Ground lilies did not usually appear until the Gale Moon. Searching upward, Alvie found the evening's first star. A sliver of moon stood fixed in the sky.

A small stone cottage caught Alvie's eye. Although its windows were darkened, 'twas obviously well-cared for. A stone well matching the cottage stood next to the dwelling and next to that was a wooden bench. Alvie walked to the bench and ran his hand over it. A scene had been lovingly chiseled into the wood. He couldn't make out everything being illustrated in the twilight, but the carved shapes of trees, deer, and the moon stood out.

Kenn had trotted to the cottage and stood next to the door. Almost as if he recognized this place. Encouraging. The mule munched on ground lilies.

Behind him, he heard approaching steps. At first, he assumed it would be the hoshefer, but instead, Alvie found a short, ancient man coming out of the trees carrying something rounded like a boulder. The man's long white beard dangled over a long tunic bearing more holes than any tunic Alvie had ever worn, which seemed quite the feat.

"What in the name of all that is stars-forsaken are you doing here?" the man shouted. His voice was rough, like scratching chalk across a piece of slate. He marched toward Alvie in a manner that left no doubt that Alvie was unwelcome. Very unwelcome.

Alvie stood dumbly. "Uh."

When the man was in front of Alvie, almost a head shorter, he glared up at him with menacing eyes. Alvie found 'twas better to focus on the ground.

"Are you hard of hearing or merely a twit? What are you doing here?"

Alvie didn't need to ask if this man was the Cibil. Somehow, he'd sensed it when meeting his eyes. "Uh, I, uh, brought you Kenn."

"Kenn?"

As if he'd been waiting for his moment, the grey stallion trotted to the Cibil and nuzzled his former master.

The Cibil's shoulders relaxed at the sight of Kenn. He set down the bundle in his arms, and stroked Kenn's nose, whispering to the horse for a moment before turning back to Alvie.

"What fool called him Kenn?"

"Sloane did," Alvie said before adding, "sir."

"Oh." At Sloane's name, the Cibil's face softened. "Well, the Unsung . . ." He trailed off and Alvie didn't press him to continue.

Where Sloane was concerned, one could write volumes and yet, Alvie, himself, still had difficulty expressing his own feelings of grief. He didn't know if the Cibil grieved—he didn't know Sloane— but Alvie had always wondered what the Cibil *really* knew when he'd sent Sloane to Ayla to retrieve the "weapon" from the goddess of the Azure Moon.

"His name is Galdefinness."

"Who?"

"The horse." The Cibil pursed his lips as if stopping himself from calling Alvie 'twit' again.

"Galda-what? What kind of horse's name is that?"

"A much better one than Kenn." The Cibil didn't take his horse's reins, but Kenn followed him like a pup as he collected the large round item he'd placed on the ground and strode to a wooden shed next to the cottage that Alvie hadn't noticed.

The chatter in the nearby trees caused both men to turn toward the noise. When no further noises sounded, the Cibil eyed Alvie with a raised brow.

"Hmm," he said before opening the door to the shed and stepping inside.

The door swung shut behind him, but it didn't quite latch. Galda–

Kenn whinnied in irritation but then joined the mule in devouring ground lilies instead.

Alvie swung his arms to and fro, uncertain of what he should do. After waiting a half-hour's time for the Cibil to exit and becoming increasingly bored, Alvie walked to the shed.

Should he knock?

"Master Cibil, I don't mean to intrude, but—"

He paused.

Inside, the Cibil was . . . was he sobbing? There was a definite sort of moaning sound from within. Alvie pressed his ear to the crack in the door. Aye, it had to be.

Filled with embarrassment for encroaching on the Cibil's private moment, Alvie retreated. At that same moment, the door flung open, revealing the Cibil holding the same boulder-like object from before.

"Leave," the Cibil said quietly. "You are not supposed to be here. You're *early.*"

Alvie stared at the darkened ground so he didn't meet the glossy eyes of the Cibil. "I'm sorry."

Neither moved.

"What do you mean 'early?'"

"Look up." The Cibil pointed into the air. "You see the moon there? You're early."

"I'm sorry. I got lost, as it were, gettin' here—you know, Kage Duna is not an easy place to get around—and then I didn't really know what night it was, you know? I just sort of got here. Wait!" Alvie caught a better view of what the Cibil held. "Is that . . . a turtle, Master Cibil?"

The Cibil gazed down at the round creature in his arms. Even in the shadowed light of nighttime, Alvie noted that the turtle's shell reflected a lustrous hue. Rather than the muted greens, browns, or greys of a usual turtle's shell, this one appeared to be turquoise.

What was more, elaborate iridescent swirls covered it. Alvie's nose scrunched, wracking his brain.

"What sort of turtle is that?" Alvie asked, choosing to keep his eyes on the incandescent shell rather than the Cibil. "And why isn't it moving?"

"'Tis dead." The Cibil's voice was flat, but something made Alvie meet his gaze.

If anyone understood loss, 'twas Alvie. This turtle had been the Cibil's friend, or pet, or something.

"Now leave."

"But—"

"Leave. And do not return." The Cibil carried the dead turtle into his cottage, and this time, slammed and bolted the door behind him.

IF THE CIBIL HAD REAPPEARED THAT NIGHT, HE would not have been the first person who explained to Alvie that he was a poor listener. Alvie did not leave. Instead, he did what he always did if a story could not win someone over—he made himself useful.

Tired though he might be, and even as late as it was, Alvie paced the glade considering what he might do to earn a two-day stay with the Cibil. If he was reading the moon correctly, it should only be that long before the night of the Nay Moon.

He'd already noticed that the glade seemed to be protected from late winter's cold, but he also noted the cottage had a chimney and the Cibil only had a half-dozen pieces of firewood in reserve against the cottage. Blessedly, he found an ax in the shed. The ax wasn't sharpened but would do. At first, he wondered if the chopping noise would do more harm than good, but if the Cibil was seething inside his cabin at Alvie's ruckus, he did not let on. Alvie neither saw his silhouette in the window nor heard any voice from within.

As he set the last piece of firewood on the restocked pile, he brushed his sweaty brow, pleased. No one ever supposed Alvie was as strong as he was. His peg leg often kept others from noticing the muscular torso that he'd developed over the years. He often chuckled to himself when people gaped at how much he could heft. Missing a limb hadn't made Alvie weak. It had challenged him to become strong in other ways.

Alvie was certain the Cibil observed him, despite remaining from sight, and hoped he wasn't a quick judge.

'Twas difficult to say as the Cibil had been so cross. But with luck, replenished firewood would hopefully soften the man until Alvie could get a good story in. The Cibil *must* be in need of a story.

With no other chores coming to mind and with a growing number of yawns escaping him, Alvie took his bedroll from Kenn's saddle, unfurled it on the edge of the glade away from the cottage, and said a quick prayer to the Hunger Moon goddess that the Cibil would change his mind in the morning.

CHAPTER
4

The thick, slobbery tongue of the mule awoke Alvie in the next morning.

"Oi!" He jumped up, balancing on his foot. He'd slipped off his peg leg before going to sleep as he usually did. "Get out of here!" He shoved his shoulder into the mule, who didn't budge, and his balance wobbled as he bounced off the creature's side. "Ah, you stinky goat."

Alvie sat and fastened the peg leg to his stump, buckling the leather strap that Sloane had made for him snug and secure. This strap was the greatest gift that Alvie had ever received—with a close second being the starstone club Sir Tolvar had given him. The strap had changed his life. No longer did Alvie end his days with his stump rope-burned and raw. To be able to begin his days without the dread of imminent pain was a wonder.

He didn't discern the Cibil anywhere but didn't know if he still kept to the cottage or had left the glade.

Kenn was gone.

Alvie panicked momentarily before deciding that mayhap the Cibil had ridden off with the stallion somewhere. Kenn was the old man's horse, after all, even if Alvie had decided that there was no way he'd be able to call him anything but Kenn. He had another moment of panic about his supplies, most of which had been in Kenn's saddlebags, before seeing the bags on the ground next to the well. And still a third moment, wondering if the Cibil would return before the Nay Moon.

"But 'course he will. Where does he have to go?"

Alvie chewed on the last of the hardtack, not daring to see what food the Cibil might have. He did, however, help himself to ladles full of the fresh well water.

He was still filthy and caked with dried mud, but Alvie wouldn't concern himself about that now.

"Right then." What else could Alvie do to help the Cibil? He would not intrude into the cottage, but mayhap the shed could use tidying.

The door creaked open, and Alvie braced himself for either a tongue-wagging or a thumping or both. But the shed was void of anyone. Not empty though. Stacks of dusty parchments, jars of who knew what, and a keg barrel of rusty tools stood there. And those were merely the first items Alvie glanced at. There was a wooden counter with about two feet of empty space on it, but other than that, the shed was bursting with *things*.

Alvie rolled up his sleeves. This was better than better. This was perfect. Who didn't want a little thorough cleaning every now and again?

The Cibil, apparently.

When the Cibil returned leading Kenn late that afternoon, Alvie watched in dismay as the ancient man thrashed around the half-cleaned shed. Choice words escaped his mouth as his face went scarlet.

"What in stars' name were you thinking?"

"I was thinking I was helpin' you." Alvie scratched the back of his head, scanning the boxes and crates that were still strewn around the outside of the shed.

"Helping me? Helping me? Did I ask for your help?"

"Nay, but—"

"Are you always this vexing?"

If Alvie was honest, 'twas not the first time someone had said something like this to him. He scanned the mess he'd created. He was only trying to help.

The Cibil hoisted a crate off the ground and marched it into the shed. When he exited and surveyed Alvie's unfinished scattered mess, he sighed, strode to his cottage and slammed the door.

Two door slammings. That wasn't good.

Deciding it might be best for him to give the Cibil some more space, Alvie loped out of the glade and into the trees where the Cibil had come from. It wasn't long before he came out of the trees and stumbled upon a giant lake.

Alvie stared dumbfounded at the sight. A lake in the middle of Kage Duna? Surrounded completely by trees, at least the shores that Alvie could see, the lake was crystal clear and blue. It was mesmerizing.

After a moment, Alvie stripped off his tunic and scrubbed the filthy item on the banks, leaving it off to dry before splashing himself in the clear water. That done, he walked the perimeter of the lake in the warm sunshine, stopping every so often to gaze into its depths to see if it held fish. That certainly would beat hardtack—not that Alvie had any of that left, he remembered. Stars, what would he eat for supper?

Oh well. He'd gone hungry plenty of times before, and he likely would again. He'd figure something out. He always had. If anything, he could eat a few of the ground lilies the mule had taken a liking to. They had a terrible bitterness, but as he'd discovered years ago, they were edible for people.

Alvie didn't know how long he'd skimmed the perimeter of the lake, but by evening, he'd made it straight to the opposite side. He shrugged on his mostly dry tunic and spent a moment surveying the area. His stomach growled and, following its cue, he decided to walk back. Hopefully, the mule had left some ground lilies for him.

His next step caused his peg leg to sink into a sludgy spot in the dirt, throwing him off-balance.

"What the—?" Alvie attempted to lift his peg leg, but it was good and stuck. Grabbing onto the wooden peg, Alvie wrenched it out of the gunk, splattering mud on his face as he did so.

"Blah." He coughed mud out of his mouth, trying to wipe his face but failing as his hands were covered in the grey stuff.

It appeared to be like the mud of the swamps he'd traveled through in Kage Duna. Pivoting, Alvie noticed that behind him, the grey mud continued into the trees, which sagged and appeared to have dried, dead leaves hanging from their branches. In the other direction, toward the lake, the sludge continued to the banks and into the water.

Careful to not walk directly in the mud and become stuck again, Alvie bent at the waist to more closely examine the lake in this spot. The sludge leaking from this bank colored the water yards into the pristine lake.

It almost seemed to stain the lake.

"Blimey," Alvie said, touching the water. His hand came out grey and covered in mud rather than wet and sandy as he'd assumed it would. As it should. He touched it again. Aye, not wet with water's drips, caked with sludge.

He stopped himself from scratching his head with his filthy hand but stood and assessed the stain this mud created.

"I wonder if it'll eventually cover the lake," Alvie said to himself.

"It will. I estimate in about two moons," the answer came.

The Cibil stepped out from the trees and stood next to Alvie. He stared into the lake.

"What's happening here?" Alvie asked. "How does this lake even exist? What's gonna happen when it's covered by the swamp? Does this have something to do with the Befallen?"

The last question had escaped before Alvie could consider what he had asked. He gave the Cibil an expression of dread.

The Cibil's expression seemed intended to be a slight close-lipped smile. What he actually offered was a sour look of annoyance. "Certainly are full of questions, aren't you?"

"Fact o'matter, 'tis not every day you come across something like this."

The Cibil was quiet, letting dusk fall over the lake. "Nay, you do not. And to answer your last question first, nay, this has naught to do with the Befallen."

Alvie exhaled. "Whew. Well, that is somethin', anyway."

"But unless this can be stopped, I shall lose my home. This lake has been here for centuries, and *I* with it. I do not belong elsewhere. If I cannot hail here . . ." The Cibil shook his head. "I suppose I am old enough. The world may not require my existence any longer. And yet—" His head turned east. Alvie followed suit, squinting into the trees.

"Are you Seeing the future?" Alvie asked.

"Too many questions and too ignorant for words." The Cibil began shuffling in the direction of his glade. Alvie fell into step with him.

"I'm very sorry, Master Cibil. I just wanted to return Kenn to you—"

"Galdefinness."

"Aye, that's what I meant. Galdufeenus. And go on an adventure, I s'pose. I've traveled m'whole life, but until I met Sloane, never had a proper adventure, you know? Now I'm gonna be in the Order of Siria and I know Ghlee's takin' a liking to me, but fact o'matter, I want to feel like a real knight."

They'd walked for a quarter-hour before the Cibil said, "You were a great help to her, Alvie, son of Alva of Kestriel. She could not have been the Unsung without you."

Alvie felt heartened at the sentiment. He didn't comment on the Cibil using his name, which he had not given him, nor the use of his father's name. Even Alvie knew when to be quiet.

He really is magic, this Cibil.

"Can you cook?"

"Oi?"

"Can you cook?" the Cibil asked more impatiently this time.

"Oh, aye. 'Course. I'm not as good as Lauge," Alvie said, referring to the only man who had made Alvie part of his family—before Sloane, of course, "But, aye. I can cook."

"Very well. Let us test that then when we return."

"'TIS EDIBLE," THE CIBIL REMARKED OF ALVIE'S STEW.

Truly, Alvie hadn't been given too much to work with besides a bushel of mushrooms and some tins of herbs. And mushrooms were not Alvie's favorite ingredient. What he could have used was the little jar of spices he had left back at Dara Keep. He would have been able to make a proper stew. This stew tasted like how Alvie imagined the forest floor would taste. But if neither man particularly loved the mushroom stew, it didn't stop their appetites, as they both had three bowls of the stuff. Alvie was relieved when the Cibil helped himself to a second and third bowl, silently giving him permission to do the same.

During their meal, Alvie attempted to entertain the Cibil with a few stories, but when even his comedic tale of becoming a beekeeper for a single day fell flat, Alvie stared into his bowl and joined the Cibil in silence.

Or tried to.

The questions kept coming. How long had the Cibil lived here? (He did not ask how old he was: that would be impolite.) Did he ever miss having company? (He did not ask if Sloane had been his last company: that would make Alvie sad.) Was he thrilled to have Gala . . . Gadla . . . Gaydlah . . . Kenn back? (He did not bring up how the Cibil had "lost" Kenn: that would make the Cibil sad.)

To each question, the Cibil remained silent, but at least he had not thrown Alvie a scowl or stalked away to his cottage.

Finally, Alvie asked, "Master Cibil, do you know what is causing the occurrence at the lake?"

The Cibil pursed his lips in thought. "I do."

Alvie's brows rose in excitement that the Cibil had *finally* bestowed him with an answer. "Can you tell me?"

The Cibil stood and entered his cottage. Alvie's heart sank.

Preparing to hear the door slam a third time, he was surprised when the Cibil came out carrying a burlap bundle. He sat next to Alvie and unwrapped it. 'Twas the shimmery dead turtle.

"'Tis the sindri turtles."

"A turtle is causin' that?"

A throaty sound from the Cibil told Alvie to be quiet. "The *lack* of sindri turtles is the cause." He lifted his eyes to Alvie. "The lake is a natural phenomenon that, as you have no doubt noticed from observing the rest of Kage Duna, should not exist. Deogol may have an extraordinary and curious geological makeup, but a swampland should remain a swampland."

Alvie nodded, waiting for the Cibil to go on.

"But the sindri turtles, whose natural habitat are the foothills of the southern Monas Territory, have migrated here for centuries, even before I made this place my home. They migrate six moons after they hatch and make the lake their home."

Alvie bit his lip so he did not interrupt.

The Cibil paused, making Alvie sit in his patience. "Sindri turtles are special, as you can plainly see from this shell. First, their shells—and their eggshells, I might add—are notoriously resilient. Almost unbreakable. Even more remarkable is the fact that their shells reflect light. Light of the moon and light of the stars. One might say they reflect *my* light. Moreover, the sindri turtles eat the algae that grows on the bottom of the lake. 'Tis what makes the lake so pristine."

Alvie gazed at the dead turtle.

The Cibil nodded. "Aye, the turtles have died off. But even still, there should be young sindris in the lake. There are none."

"Can't they just hatch babies here?"

Rather than giving him an expression of agitation, the Cibil appeared pleased by Alvie's question. "You might think that, but nay. When the time comes to mate, the sindris migrate back to the Monas Territory where *they* hatched and lay their eggs in the same place before journeying back here."

"That's a lot of rubbish. Seems like there's fine spots by the lake to lay eggs."

The Cibil's eyes twinkled. "Who can explain the creatures of nature? While that would certainly be easiest for them, they must follow their instincts. Unfortunately, the turtles have ceased to migrate altogether over the last five years."

"So . . . but you said it wasn't the Befallen." Alvie couldn't help himself. The Befallen had first appeared in Deogol five years ago. *Anyone* in the kingdom knew that.

Was it so difficult to believe that the two were intertwined?

"The Befallen itself isn't necessarily what stopped the turtles from migrating. 'Tis something else. But that doesn't mean they do not connect."

"What do you mean?"

"I have some theories, but no solid answer."

"Oh."

"Aye, 'oh.'" The Cibil studied the hint of moon above. "I suppose you'll still be here tomorrow, given 'tis the Nay Moon. If you are still willing, I have a dozen tools in need of cleaning."

Alvie nodded.

"Good night, Alvie," the Cibil said as he rose to go to his cottage. "Count yourself fortunate. You may be the last person who ever asks me a question."

CHAPTER
5

Now that the Cibil had cracked the doorway of potential—well, not friendship exactly, but rapport nevertheless, Alvie was determined to ensure that door wouldn't slam a third time on him.

He spent the morning cleaning and polishing tools: a spade, a hoe, a rake with half the tines broken off, a scythe (though Alvie had not the faintest idea what the Cibil would use it for), and some other tools that appeared to be as old as the Cibil, which they probably were. The ax Alvie devoted a great deal of time to sharpening, a frustrating task as the Cibil's sharpening stone was miniscule and worn.

When the noon sun stood high, Alvie meandered to the lake to wash off his filthy hands and arms. While he could wash using the well water, he wanted to take another gander at the lake.

The clear blue side greeted him benignly. Alvie scanned for any sign of a turtle swimming about. The lake remained smooth like glass.

Why *were* those turtles not migrating here any longer?

Alvie was not one to oft give thought to the unexplainable things in life. 'Twas one reason why he had found drifting around Deogol simple. When the Cors fever took his leg, his family, and his everything, he figured out life without those things. When work dried up in one town, he simply found another that provided opportunity.

When prayers to the moon goddesses went unanswered, he ceased to pray. There was naught so consequential that Alvie had not been able to accept and march on.

Except now that he had been through an adventure with Sloane and had witnessed faith up close, he *had* begun to make prayers to the goddesses, hadn't he?

They weren't proper prayers to Alvie's mind. More like small conversations in which Alvie explained to the goddesses that he missed Sloane, or how he wasn't sure if he should go with Ghlee or return to Branwell with Lauge.

And now, he'd met the Cibil of the Nay Moon. The ancient man may have attempted to keep his words vague, but 'twas clear to Alvie that he fretted about what would happen to him if the lake became fully sullied. Would it dry up the well? Alvie had lived without a great deal in life, but no one could live without water.

And what had the Cibil meant when he'd said, *"the world may not require my existence any longer?"*

It couldn't mean what Alvie suspected, could it?

When Alvie returned to the glade, he froze. The Cibil held his starstone club and was inspecting it through a pair of thick spectacles. Alvie came to stand next to him; the Cibil shot a look over the top of his spectacles.

"Well, well, you are full of surprises. How did you come by this?"

"'Twas a gift, sir."

"A timely one."

Alvie grimaced in confusion but did not ask any questions as the Cibil shuffled off into his cottage. Alvie wondered if the starstone club had just been swiped out from under him, but again, kept quiet as the Cibil shut his door.

When the door opened in the evening, Alvie held his breath until he spotted the club in the Cibil's hand. Alvie had built a cookfire and made more mushroom stew for lack of anything else to cook. The Cibil seemed pleased as he sat, placed the club between the two, and accepted a bowl from Alvie.

Just two more hours until the Nay Moon began.

Alvie gave him a side-glance, in awe that the old man should still remain silent. Goddesses of the moon, it certainly was difficult being in the Cibil's quiet presence. Lauge may chide Alvie, but he had never felt he needed to be quite so noiseless. He was ready to burst with stories, jokes, and questions.

The Cibil appeared unaware of Alvie's predicament but soundlessly spooned his stew into his mouth, not focused on anything in particular.

"Your gift there." The Cibil eyed the club. "It has a long line of keepers. Would you like to know more?"

Alvie didn't need to be asked twice. "Aye! I should love that!"

"Hmph. That stone your friend had—"

"The Edan Stone?" asked Alvie, referring to the magical stone that had both led Sloane to the Befallen and also kept the possessor safe from the effects of that dark curse. His friend, Sir Tolvar, possessed the stone now.

"Aye, the stone. This club is its antithesis. Whereas the Edan Stone is the moon. Shadows. Starstone is the light of the stars incarnate. 'Tis why it is so rare. How it came here from the heavens, there are very few remaining accounts, all conflicting. I have read that a half-dozen pieces of starstone exist on the continent, but only three have tales giving real evidence of their existence. The most famous of these tales is of a foregone champion, a knight you could say, although 'twas ere our time of modern-day knighthoods.

"This champion was called the Night Caller. 'Twas the greatest warrior who e'er existed. And he wielded an unstoppable weapon. A club guised as wood, deceiving those who mocked it. The Night Caller defeated anyone who challenged him. Yet, he was just, too. A hero to an early people who suffered at the hand of any tormentor greedy enough to take power. Legends speculate 'twas he who discovered and buried the original traces of the Curse of Adrienne."

Alvie shuddered at the word 'Adrienne' while at the same time being impressed that the Cibil did not. The word itself was cursed.

"Long ago, before the Mehr Sea was called such. Before the existence of the mighty Capella Realm, or the StarSeers, or any kingdom boundaries dotted any map, Tasia was dark."

"Dark?"

"Aye. The sun could not yet settle all its light on the continent. Daylight was limited to scant days of faint, streaming sunlight as if through a haze. And night was not what 'tis now, either. The moon was screened in the shadowed canvas, and only the boldest of stars broke through the blind shuttering the sky. 'Twas dark. And night was hated and feared.

"But the source of that darkness—the *blind*—was not night, as so many assumed, but a Curse surrounding the continent. It halted the light of the sun, moon, and stars from blessing Tasia. Dismay veiled the air. But the Night Caller—before he was called so—knew from studying the dim light of the stars that all was not as it seemed.

"Then, to his amazement, one night, a singular star spoke to him. Light was there. Above, beyond the blind, 'twas there. He suspected then that the darkness did not belong to the night, as it was believed, but to a source no one could fathom. And if Light came from above, even at night, then the darkness came from elsewhere and must, too, have a source.

"He wasted no time. He started out that very night and journeyed for years—before time was measured as such—searching for the source of the darkness. Unbeknownst to him, he searched for Adrienne itself. He found the Curse in traces marking the earth like scattered veins and followed. It led him to what is now known as the Skyward Mountains and down into a valley that is widely unknown to even the most apt of mapmakers."

Alvie lifted a single eyebrow but did not interrupt.

"There, he discovered a cave. The very bottom of the cave seemed dipped in oozy darkness.

"He felt it there. The source of the darkness. Adrienne.

"The force of Adrienne attempted to draw him to it. It almost succeeded. But before it could entwine him in its traces, he managed to escape. He raced through the land, searching for others to join him. To fight it. Defeat it. But few believed, and no one dared to join him. Fear is powerful.

"The stories conflict on how the Night Caller came to have the starstone club. Some say it was tears of Light sent from the stars and gathered in a pool. Some say that he dipped a simple wooden club into a pool of impossible starlight. But there is another account that tells how the Night Caller prayed for the course of an entire moon and when he finally stood, the starstone had simply materialized. Whatever it was that brought him that starstone, it gave him a power lent by the stars. A power to wield the Light of Siria."

Alvie gazed down at the club, remembering the thug who had possessed it before Sir Tolvar had taken it and passed it to him. "But one of the Brones had this. Are you sayin' he had the Light of Siria?"

"Of course not!" the Cibil chided. "Starstone itself is little more than a metal. Strong, aye, but through it, and through a hero's faith, the stars worked their power. Now listen."

Alvie nodded.

"With his new weapon, the Night Caller began to raise forces. And raise hope. Night became less feared. The starstone became a symbol of night's Light. Yet, a battle no one was prepared for was brewing. As he gathered those who had a belief in Light, so too, Adrienne had a way of drawing and collecting the weak and corrupt. Those who would be susceptible to the darkness. Manipulated by the trace of Adrienne, they believed they could use that darkness for their own means. But as you've discovered, Adrienne cannot be controlled.

"A battle erupted. And in a harrowing fray, the Night Caller was captured. The starstone was taken from him. His execution set. Imprisoned in an underground cell, there was little for him to do but pray. When he'd prayed to every unseen star in the sky, he prayed to the unseen sun to strengthen its light. And when he was too exhausted to pray further, he prayed still. To the full moon in the sky. He offered a bargain. His life for another. His life for a *new* champion who could lead the hopeful into the dawn, into the sun, into a world filled with Light, not darkness.

"'Twas then that he was visited in his cell by the goddess of the Rainless Moon. So moved was she by his willingness to sacrifice himself and to seek no glory that she deemed him a hero. She offered him a pair of midnight gloves."

"What are—"

"Midnight gloves fashioned from a patch of the night sky itself. And told him that with these gloves, he would bury the Curse. She then held out a perfect, glowing orb, a sphere of cinth, and told him to press his palms upon its surface. He did. He vanished from his cell and found himself standing on a mountain top, holding his starstone club in one hand and the midnight gloves in the other, and peering down at the valley that held the cave.

"He truly understood then Night's majesty and the balance of its own exquisite darkness that could ne'er be likened to Adrienne. He placed the gloves on his hands and soon stepped into the cave."

"'Tis unclear all that occurred in that cave. But at dawn, the sun rose. A morning sun such as never had been experienced before. A sun no longer concealed by the blind. A golden light cascaded across a clear, crisp sky. All who gazed upon it wept to see such a brilliant dawn.

"The sky was no longer grey and hazed by the blind, but blue.

"A hero emerged from the cave, battered. His arm was oiled black. But he still wore the gloves and held his weapon. Victorious. Adrienne had been buried.

"The rest of his days, the Night Caller spent wreaking havoc upon those who sought to challenge the Light. As I said before, he was a warrior for the good. Beloved."

The Cibil paused and the two peered up at the velvet sky above.

"I imagine that first night when the world gazed up to see the stars no longer masked by the blind might be the most wondrous moment Tasia has ever experienced. And 'twas that first night that the goddess of the Rainless Moon honored him with a hero's title, Night Caller."

"Blimey."

As Alvie pondered the last of the Cibil's story, picturing the valiant warrior's life purpose as a protector of others, something swelled inside. He envisioned himself battling dark villains, defending innocent orphans (not so unlike himself long ago) and elders who may no longer be able to uphold their own securities, like Lauge.

Or the Cibil.

Aye, like the Cibil. If the lake became malignant and the Cibil was forced from Kage Duna, how would that ancient man survive?

The world needs the Cibil. Despite what the old man had said.

Mayhap the Cibil could return to Dara Keep with Alvie? Certainly, the fortification of the Order of Siria would be safe. But the Cibil was scarcely able to endure Alvie's company—and he was a pleasure to have around. The Cibil seemed awfully adamant that he preferred his own company.

Well, if the Cibil couldn't return home with Alvie, Alvie would just have to return the Cibil's home to him.

"Master Cibil, I want to help you. I'm going to find out why them sindri turtles ceased migratin' here. I'm going to return them, sir."

The Cibil didn't meet Alvie's eyes, nor did he acknowledge the younger man. The only indication that the Cibil had heard Alvie at all was the ever-so-slight side curl of his lip.

Alvie began silently counting in his mind so he would not say anything else.

By now, night had made her quiet entrance and, true to this eve's darkness, no moon revealed itself. The stars delicately silhouetted the tree branches above them.

"And now the Nay Moon is upon us," the Cibil intoned. "Beware. One question is all you are permitted. And I see many questions inside you. If you are to uncover the mystery of the sindri turtles' disappearance, where will you begin? If you find where they have gone, how will you return them? How will you make certain they do not disappear again? What dangers lay in the way? Can you, Alvie, do this all alone?"

At that question, Alvie barked out a laugh.

"Beg your pardon, Master Cibil, but I ain't so afraid of doin' anything alone."

"Hmph. That is good. Yet you may find you need help before the end. Mayhap it shall come from a source you least expect."

Alvie's brows knit together. He almost asked, "What do you mean by that?" but the Cibil wasn't going to trick him.

"Right then. I s'pose I'll just begin north in those foothills. The Monas Territory ain't too far away. Naught but a few days, I reckon. But I better get started right away. Don't want that lake to become noxious, you know? Although it shouldn't take me two moons, I wager. Fact o'matter, I wager I'll return before the next Nay Moon." During this speech, Alvie had stood, gone to his saddle bags, and rummaged through them. He mentally made a list of what he needed. There were a few items he would need to borrow—all right, take— from the Cibil, but he wasn't too concerned. "Don't you worry, Master Cibil. I'll return those lil' turtles. You'll get your lake back."

He glanced between Kenn and the mule. Kenn was certainly the more majestic of the two animals. If Kenn was a noble knight, the mule was an oafish jester. But people who did not know mules did not understand their quality. Despite their stubbornness, mules were hardy creatures, sure-footed, and required less food. Kenn looked the part, but suddenly, Alvie was delighted the Order had sent him off with the mule.

The hairs on the back of his neck stood on end.

Nah. 'Tis got to be a coincidence.

Without asking the Cibil, Alvie placed some of the ancient man's belongings in the mule's saddlebags, a small old pick he'd found among all the Cibil's rusted tools, a healthy length of rope, sacks of dried mushrooms and apples, and a tiny pouch of salt—that made the Cibil glare at him. Then Alvie filled his water skins with well water. He bridled and saddled the mule, who stood unamused, but patient, nevertheless.

All the while, no other words had been said between either man. But when Alvie faced the Cibil again, surprise was plain on the old man's face. Alvie almost let out a laugh—the expression had to be a rarity, indeed—but he did not want to offend the Cibil.

The expression disappeared and the Cibil's solemn eyes peered into Alvie's own. Was that merriment just beneath the surface?

"Well, I'll be off then," Alvie said, and tugged at the mule's lead. "Come on, you ol' goat." The thrill of adventure hung in the still air. He led the mule to the edge of the glade.

"You're leaving *now*?"

"Aye. Just like the Night Caller." Alvie beamed.

"Hmph."

Alvie had taken a few more steps when the Cibil called once more behind him. "You did not ask a question."

Alvie halted, the mule's muzzle bumping into his backside. He turned to the Cibil, fighting the grin bursting from him. "When I come back, can I have a hero's title?"

For the second time, the Cibil shot him an expression of incredulity. Then, he shook his head. If Alvie didn't know any better, he could have sworn the Cibil was chuckling under his breath.

"Aye. If you fulfill your quest, you'll have your hero's title."

CHAPTER
6

The air smelled *much* better now that Alvie was in the Monas Territory. He'd crossed the border of Kage Duna two days ago and had been forced to cut through the sand-riddled landscape of The Mort only briefly. Thankfully, 'twas the wrong time of year for the infamous dust storms that plagued the area. But the dusty scent of overly dried and dead plants had lingered, making Alvie cover his nose with the collar of his tunic while he traveled there. The mule had sidestepped its way through The Mort easily, negotiating past any haste-sand traps that Alvie might have missed were he walking.

Nevertheless, Alvie had wanted to kiss the ground when they'd finally made it to the rocky terrain of the Monas Territory. He spent an hour removing sand from the mule's coarse mane, under the saddle, the sleeves of his tunic, his shoe, and even under the leather strap of his peg leg.

"Blah." Alvie spat dust. "There has to be another way when we return."

The mule snorted in reply.

Alvie nodded, digging sand out of his ear.

"I just realized this is the furthest north I ever been," Alvie said. "I suppose for you, too."

The mule tilted its neck away.

"Well, you need not be like that." Alvie brushed off his hose, taking in their new scenery. The purple twilight hit the giant boulders at the bottom of the foothills, painting everything in shades of blue and grey. Ahead, and on either side as far as Alvie could detect, the foothills were a mix of smooth rock walls and jagged crags jutting up into the sky, resembling spires one might see on some ancient temple to the goddesses of the moon. No road existed, but time had worn away the rugged earth in places and Alvie imagined that a path might exist for a creature like the mule, who had sense where to place his hooves.

But for sindri turtles? How in stars' name would they travel all the way from wherever their birthing ground was down these craggy foothills and reach the lake at Kage Duna?

Alvie peered this way and that, attempting to envision being a little turtle with a mad quest to procreate in what had to be the dumbest way possible.

Who can explain the creatures of nature? That is what the Cibil had said.

He supposed he couldn't concern himself too much with the why. Indeed, who could explain the nature of some humans? What made some people kind and others full of detestation? Some were brave, some were cowards. When Alvie really considered it, humans had the greatest opportunity to be the best of nature and the worst. They weren't sindri turtles, innocently—albeit nonsensically—following the same path nature had set. Nay, humans had an infinite number of choices placed before them and for whatever reason, some just plain took to a bad path.

But Alvie was determined to be a hero and earn that hero's title.

"Come on, you ol' goat. Let's see what's this way." Alvie tugged at the mule's rope and the animal followed.

When 'twas too dark to continue—Alvie wasn't going to test

either his or the mule's sure-footedness to that extreme—he settled them in for the night. He longed for a cookfire—as much for its warmth as for any other reason—but there wasn't enough wood to make even a miniscule fire.

Besides, what would I cook?

He sat on the ground, which was actually a giant smooth rock, and wrapped his blanket around himself, missing the bizarre warmth of the Cibil's glade. His stump ached and Alvie weighed the decision of taking off his peg leg. If he should need to quickly arise, he wanted to be ready. He gave in to his discomfort and removed it, massaging his stump and the muscles around his kneecap in relief. His rear already ached from the mule and the rock gave no relief to his backside. Sleeping on a rock wouldn't be a first, but the fact of the matter was Alvie liked the comfort of a bed same as anyone.

A soft cot awaited him at Dara Keep, and he smiled in the darkness.

Under the sliver of moon, the sparse sagemary bushes appeared as small animals, although Alvie hadn't seen anything today except for brown stone lizards—some the size of a hound, others, the size of his fist.

When he'd begun his new journey, he'd recalled the hoshefer and half-wondered if it would come out of hiding and follow him again. But he had not spotted it while traipsing back through damp Kage Duna and of course, 'twould never have followed him through The Mort. Never.

"S'pose it returned to Ayla or wherever it lived."

Alvie didn't remember falling asleep, but the rising sun's jabs at his closed eyelids as it poked over the mountains awoke him with a start. He shivered, puffs of breath visibly hanging. His blanket lay rumpled next to him.

Shivering, Alvie sat up and fastened his peg leg tight to his stump before standing and folding the blanket. "You makin' breakfast this morning?" he asked the mule, who, too, squinted in the dawn as it stood over the sagemary bush it had obviously been munching.

"Fine. S'pose it'll be me again." He withdrew a few mushrooms out of the saddlebag and sighed, directing his attention back to the sagemary. Its earthy scent caught Alvie's nose. "Is that stuff any good?"

'TWAS NOT EXACTLY AIMLESS. HE HAD A PURPOSE, of course. Moving along a switchback trail he made up as they journeyed, Alvie was surprised when he peered down. They had made it a few hundred feet up the foothills. The mule did not share his excitement but did not seem troubled to continue either. For the most part, Alvie had led the mule rather than ride him. He wanted to wait until it became absolutely necessary. He'd managed to slip only two or three times, his peg leg losing balance on slick spots in the rock.

But after midday, Alvie was finally forced onto the mule. Along the rims of narrow cliffs, the mule trotted along, unconcerned with the fact that naught but chilly air was at his side. Alvie ignored his racing heart and fought to keep his mushroom meal down.

'Twas late afternoon, when they came upon the gulch. Sheer walls on either side stretched to the top of where Alvie could see. But the slope into the gulch, where Alvie and the mule stood, was so gradual that even a small child could walk into it easily. Best of all, a small stream flowed through it.

At the stream, Alvie filled his water skins with the fresh mountain water, took a healthy gulp, and then, as the mule drank its fill as well, splashed his face. The frigid water was more of a slap than Alvie had imagined. With a shiver, he stood, scanning the area.

Surrounded by mountains on either side, the gulch was cast in early evening shadow, but it was still light enough that Alvie could discern that the stream flowed into a slight bend that ran into a small cave—a hole in the otherwise solid mountain. In the opposite direction, the gulch curved, leaving the origin from which it flowed a mystery. Alvie wiped his wet chin on his sleeve. Investigating the cave into which the stream flowed did not appeal to him. Not without a torch. He decided exploring upstream was a better choice for now.

"You stay here," he told the mule. "Guard the place." Alvie barked a laugh at his own humor and followed the stream, the banks of which grew narrower as he walked.

A sense of haste guided him—how much evening light would he have before the gulch was fully in the gloam? Rounding the bend, he heard water running before he saw the miniature waterfall tumbling from a small pool a few feet above into the stream, where Alvie now stood shin-deep. Like a basin overrun, water brimmed at the edge before trickling into the stream. But how the water poured into the pool was what baffled Alvie. From a dozen feet above that pool and what might have once been another waterfall dribbled a gradual spill of water. The rock on which it drizzled was wet and stained green.

"Definitely bigger at some point," Alvie said, inspecting it. Aye, a divot running a foot from the water's edge and lining the stream told Alvie that the stream had once been larger, also.

"Blimey, that is odd," Alvie said as the remainder of the sunlight sank, leaving him in the grey of evening.

In the morning, Alvie's stiff back moaned as much from the cold temperature as the rock he'd slept on. He rose, ready to splash stream water on his face before deciding simply gazing into the icy water was enough to wake him. He blew on his cold hands before driving them into his hips, stretching and attempting to loosen his muscles.

But surely the Night Caller had had his share of stiff mornings after sleeping on a rock. The mule did not appear stiff. Rather, the mule seemed ready for action this morning. At least, that's what Alvie told himself, noting the mule munching more sagemary bushes with enthusiasm. Desperate for something other than mushrooms and wishing to save the apples, Alvie took a bite of the plant. He immediately spit it out, rubbing his sleeve against the bitter taste on this tongue.

"So much for that."

Inspecting the pool above the stream again in the morning light, Alvie was uncertain whether or not the mule could hike quite so steep an incline. And what were his choices? Go back the way he'd come, search the cave alone and without a torch, or try and climb up to where the water was coming from, with or without the mule.

"You better not eat too many of those." Alvie frowned at the sagemary branch hanging from the mule's mouth. "Might have to last you."

Alvie weighed his options, scanning the narrow crag, determining whether or not he himself, let alone a mule, could climb up.

And the mule carried Alvie's supplies.

"Fact o'matter is, I think I'm goin' to have to leave you here," Alvie finally concluded.

Before long, he had hidden the mule's saddle and the saddlebags in more sagemary bushes to conceal them from outside eyes, strapped a heavy rucksack to his back, and hefted his starstone club in his hands.

"Well, don't go wanderin' off, Goat. Goat. I s'pose that's your name now. Right good name for you, I think. So long, Goat."

Goat flicked his ears in Alvie's direction but gave no other response.

It took but a few moments of struggling up the first few feet of the rock for Alvie to realize that his starstone club was more of a hindrance than it was likely to be of help.

"Goddesses of the moon!" he exclaimed, examining the club in indecision. "A hero must have a weapon."

But it seemed improbable that he would need a weapon in finding and recovering sindri turtles. What could possibly live in these mountains that would be that dangerous? The only creatures Alvie had encountered were stone lizards.

But then, could he leave this priceless item in a sagemary bush like a discarded walking stick?

"'Tis disguised, I s'pose. Being that it looks like wood and all. What do you think?"

The mule brayed with what felt like worry.

"I know. That's why I'm concerned."

There was nothing for it. Alvie couldn't scale the rock while holding the club, and there was no way to properly attach it to the rucksack without fear of dropping and losing it. Not to mention, it'd impede his balance. His peg leg had had enough trouble in those first few feet.

He tucked it under a group of bushes closest to where the bank ended before the stream was whisked into the cave. Here, hopefully, the club would be most out of sight should someone stumble upon this area. He surveyed it when he was a bit farther away and was pleased that he could not spot the club. That was the most he could hope for. A hero had to take chances.

CHAPTER 7

A rotten day could mean so many things. It could mean having a leg amputated at age five after having the Cors fever, mere weeks after being orphaned by the same disease. It could mean coming home to his uncle's flat as a small boy and finding a group of towering men inside informing him that his uncle was dead, and he now had no remaining family and no place to live. It could mean being chased through the streets of Kestriel by older and tougher children until he had no idea where he was and how to return to the alley with the crate he'd been sleeping in for the past fortnight. It could mean being turned down for employment over and over again because someone didn't like the look of a peg leg. It could mean being an unlikely fighter in the battle of his life—*everyone's* lives, really—winning against all odds, looking around to celebrate with his best friend and then finding out she'd died.

Whenever Alvie considered whether or not he was having a rotten day, he always cataloged the rottenest days he'd had. So as to not feel sorry for himself. To remind himself that he'd had some pretty rotten days and whatever today was, it could not compare.

Therefore, when Alvie examined his bleeding palms, knee, and elbow, he was grateful that today had not *really* been rotten. He would heal. He'd made it up over the ledge. And best of all, he always told himself, he was alive.

Alvie glanced over the edge, soaking his hands in the inch of water with relief. He couldn't glimpse Goat, but he hadn't heard any noise from that direction all day, and assumed Goat was as well as a mule standing in a gulch could be.

The distance down the cliff was certainly not more than a dozen feet, and irritation jabbed at Alvie. So many hours to get up here.

On the other hand, it had been an impossibly steep climb, wet, and had no real purchase holds. And he'd accomplished it with a peg leg. Would his friend, Sir Tolvar, the Wolf, have been able to tackle this climb with quicker success? Alvie decided, no.

His gaze pulled to his elbow. The blood seeping through his sleeve had begun to crust and stuck the gash there to his sleeve. He drew up the sleeve, wincing as it made the wound bleed anew. Well, there was no time to spend on frivolous things like scrapes. He'd heal.

Still, Alvie shivered in the dropping temperature as his heartbeat slowed, his body recovering from the exertion of the climb. His cloak was in his rucksack, but he didn't want to get it wet.

Where Alvie stood in the inch of water, his soaked foot adding to his chill, there was no bank or foliage. Only more mountains, mountain walls, and rocks. Many, many rocks.

But that was interesting, wasn't it? Aye, Alvie had been staring at rocks for what seemed an eternity now, but before him stood a pile of rocks a different hue and roughness than the reddish-brown rocks that had taunted him all day. These rocks were a charcoal color and scratchy, like a carpenter's sanding file. Rocks as big as his head lay in a mound from wall to wall, almost like a barrier. 'Twas from between these rocks that water escaped, skimming this ledge before streaming down the rock shelf and into the pool below. An avalanche, mayhap?

"Maybe," Alvie said under his breath.

One fortunate aspect of these rocks was that, as they were jagged and stacked together, they were extraordinarily uncomplicated to climb. His peg leg got caught only once and when he'd made it to the top, on the other side was a buildup of water.

"'Tis a barrier, all right."

And if you were a lil' turtle using this stream as your migration path, certainly this rocky blockage would be more than a lil' *fuss.*

It could not be a terribly big stream. The barrier was making the water deeper than it should be. In the distance, it curved to the left. That was the direction Alvie would head.

"But first, let's make a stream again."

Alvie bent to lift a rock beside his foot, bracing himself to hoist its weight and gasped when he easily brought the rock to his chest. 'Twas not light exactly, but it certainly weighed less than expected.

He tossed it into the water on the other side, the *splash* ringing in his ears after the solitary day of quiet he'd experienced.

He'd counted eight rocks before instead turning his enumeration into a song, replacing the lyrics of a folk song about ale.

"Oh, I have one rock in my hand,
and I drink—I mean, throw it down.

But now 'tis gone so I'll fill my cup—
er, hands lest I wear a frown.

Oh, I have two rocks in my hand,
and I throw them down.

But now they're gone, so I'll fill
my hands lest I wear a frown."

Pleased with his wit and charged with revived energy, Alvie continued this process until he'd removed thirty-four rocks. Wiping sweat from his brow, he inspected his work, his gaze lingering on the flow of water that now spouted from the top of the rock pile. The *sputter* of water cascading from the rock shelf below brought a smile to his lips.

A thought occurred and he climbed down to survey the stream.

"Hmm, don't want it to gush too much, I reckon. Not with Goat down there."

From above, the sound of a small rockslide drew his attention. A cloud of dust hung in the air high above the rock wall.

"Hallo?" Alvie called.

When there was no response, he shrugged before climbing the rock barrier. The water level now lowered, Alvie noticed two things. A path to the left running diagonally from the stream, the gradual incline of which led further up the mountain. And on the opposite side, the opening of a small tunnel that allowed water to pass slowly through it now that the barrier had diminished. Mayhap there was another way up or down from this location if one were very small. And a good swimmer. Certainly, the tunnel was not big enough for a man or a mule.

Was there any way to get Goat up here so he could lead or ride him through this next leg of the journey? The very thought of climbing down exhausted him.

Alvie's gaze trailed upwards once more. He had the sensation he was being watched.

"Nah."

He refocused. Certainly, he could not spend the night on a pile of jaggedy rocks or in a pool of water. There was nothing for it. Alvie would have to climb down the other side of the pile, tread the water, get wet and cold, and then take the path, hopefully to somewhere he could rest for the evening with a fire.

His eyes returned to where the dust cloud had been, and his thoughts jumped to the hidden starstone club. Mayhap he should have attempted to carry it up here.

"Fact o'matter, there's nothin' for it now."

When he'd made it to the bottom of the rock pile, he attempted to hold his rucksack above his head while treading the water, but 'twas not long before the unbalanced weight of it over his head caused him to flip backward and completely douse himself and its contents in water.

Now everything Alvie owned was soaked.

"Stars, this is goin' well." His teeth chattered as he shook his legs and wrung out his hose and tunic as best he could.

At the top of the path, Alvie's heart sank. More mountains, more mountain walls, more rocks. And a dozen yards away, two startled stone lizards slinking away. What had appeared as a trail was actually a dry streambed. Small gravelly pebbles covered the narrow ground.

Alvie shivered as the evening sun sank. So much for keeping his cloak dry. 'Twas going to be a miserable night.

THE NEXT DAY, ALVIE HIKED ALONG THE DRY streambed, taking note that although he did not always have the stream in view, its babbling current let him know it was near. He hadn't felt a gaze pressed on him today. Despite being still somewhat damp, he traveled in the warm sun at a cheerful pace, due to, in part, the discovery of the bouncing echoes his whistling caused off the rock walls above.

And then, Alvie stood still. Whereas the path's incline had been smooth maneuvering thus far, his peg leg not slipping once, suddenly, a rock wall barred him from continuing.

And 'twas much, much higher than the first cliff Alvie had spent almost a day climbing.

Some colorful phrases escaped Alvie's lips before he began scouring the area to seek an alternative path.

Nothing.

Running his fingers along the rock wall, Alvie huffed a sigh.

From what he touched and what his eyes told him, there were very few holds to be made out in the wall. Peering up, Alvie tried to gauge its height. Twice the size of the city wall of Branwell, mayhap?

"That's high."

He sat to think, popping into his mouth the remainder of the mushrooms, now soggy and tasting like dirt. He hated to finish them off, but now that they'd been dunked in water, they'd be nothing but rotting fungus soon. They certainly tasted like it already.

His wandering gaze found an impossible tree branch growing out of the side of the cliff. About twelve feet up. A truly odd sight.

How? was all Alvie could think. But a few feet higher was another. And another higher than that. And higher. *Almost* all the way to the top.

"I just need to make it to that top one," Alvie said, standing. "But how?"

His fingers skimmed the wall again. If only he had something to make holds.

The pick!

Alvie dove into his rucksack, frantically searching for the pick he'd forgotten sat at the bottom of his rucksack.

"Where are you?" he said.

After a moment's search, Alvie flipped the rucksack upside

down and its contents spilled out. Alvie rummaged through the pile on the ground. 'Twas missing.

Alvie was back on his rear; his head hung.

Had he dropped it? Lost it in the stream when his rucksack had plunged into the water?

Just in case he'd missed it, Alvie hunted for it again. Nothing.

'Twas not fair.

Abruptly, Alvie lurched to a standing position and madly clawed the wall. "'Tis not fair!"

And what to tell the Cibil? 'Twas not merely that Alvie wanted his hero's title. He wanted to earn it. He wanted to aid the Cibil.

"The Night Caller didn't give up."

And neither would Alvie.

There had to be some hold somewhere that he could use to reach the first tree branch. But after several attempts and fresh cuts on his hands to show for it, Alvie was back on the ground.

A large boulder sat next to the cliff. Could he climb on that and then jump up to the tree branch?

When Alvie stood upon it, it didn't seem likely, but no other ideas were circulating.

He spent moments balancing himself on his single foot, the peg leg held out at an angle.

"Right then. One. Two. Three." He bent his good knee, then swung his hands into the air and jumped.

Alvie slammed to the ground, his chin smashing into the rock. When he lifted his hand from his chin, he was surprised it was not soaked in blood. A few drops of blood and tiny bits of sand clung to his fingers. He was lucky he'd only skinned his chin. He opened his mouth, stretching his jaw in pain.

Giving himself a moment's reprieve to let the pain ebb, Alvie decided that he'd come *close* to the tree branch. He heaved himself up.

Back on the boulder, Alvie steadied himself, ignoring his stinging chin and throbbing limbs.

"Come on, Alvie." He exhaled, bent his aching left knee and tried again.

This time, Alvie landed on his side. A groan squeezed out of him. His eyes went in and out of focus. Stars, that fall had hurt.

He propped himself up on his elbow, his other hand gingerly pressing against his side to judge for broken ribs.

Alvie gazed at the boulder with malice. There was an old adage: *Fortune's price? Once, twice, thrice.*

But Alvie was fairly certain that his body had little else to give where any price was concerned.

Small rocks littered the ground below the boulder. Although there wasn't the slightest chance that he'd create holds in the wall by hucking rocks, it might make Alvie feel better.

"Nah." That wasn't Alvie's manner.

Again, he wished for the starstone club. Surely *that* would break up a chunk in the wall.

A noise overhead compelled Alvie to crane his neck up in time to see, and skirt, a fist-sized rock plummeting from above. The rock landed inches from where Alvie's head had been. He came out of his protective position, lowering his arms.

Eyes fixed on the cliff above, he waited for another rock to drop below. But naught came. Strange. What had made this rock fall off the edge? Another one of those stone lizards? At this point, Alvie had experienced a dozen rock slides, loose rocks shifting and falling along the steep landscape. But one rock plunging over?

He bent to examine the rock. Then Alvie started. This rock was *not* a rock. A shimmery, turquoise surface revealed that quickly. Almost a perfect sphere, Alvie turned it over and over in his palms, searching for cracks or dents. There was only a small fissure.

'Twas an egg.

"But that's impossible. An egg would have splattered into a thousand pieces."

But the Cibil said sindri turtle eggshells were tough. Mighty tough.

Alvie hugged the egg to his chest. Was there a baby turtle inside? Even if the shell endured a great drop like that, could the baby inside survive? He held the egg to his ear to listen for . . . something. Anything that might give a sign that the baby turtle inside was still alive. He heard no sound.

The shell's fissure widened and in a blink of an eye, the sound of cracking made Alvie's sore jaw drop. 'Twas hatching! 'Twas hatching!

Will it think I'm its ma?

The egg split in twain. Inside was nothing.

Alvie emitted a long, mournful breath. Nothing.

Inside, only a small, dried-up mound of something.

"Poor lil' turtle." He had nary an idea what had happened to the baby turtle inside, but one thing was certain, it had died long before being dropped off a cliff. That fact did not give Alvie heart.

Alvie lifted a piece of the shell. Stars, 'twas thick. And the inside was even more shimmery than the outside of the shell. It practically glowed, it sparkled so. One might almost mistake it for cinth, a rare and highly breakable mineral. But this shell was definitely *not* highly breakable. He ran a finger over the piece of shell. Smooth. Cold.

Cold. That made Alvie's heart sink.

"I must save these lil' turtles."

Could a sindri turtle shell chisel out a hold in the rock? Well, the shell certainly wasn't doing the turtle any good.

Alvie hesitated before hammering the piece of shell into the rock wall. A crumbling of rock slid from the notch he'd made.

"Well, I'll be." Alvie raised his arm again, ignoring the pain in his elbow, and hammered again. Within a few strikes, he'd created a hold in the rock wall. Alvie smiled his silver-tooth smile, recognizing that it'd been many days since he'd grinned. Having rubbed the back of his hand against his chin to check for more bleeding, Alvie packed up his rucksack, placing the other piece of sindri turtle shell with his belongings. He slung the rucksack on his back, and then proceeded to create another hold slightly higher.

Once he was satisfied with his first two holds, Alvie placed his left foot into the notch, pinpointed where the next notch would be created, hoisted himself up, letting his right leg hang. Since inserting the stem of his peg leg in the notches would be near impossible, Alvie was about to test just how strong his other limbs were.

He huffed out a breath and swung his arm up with the shell in his hand, striking into the rock wall. He landed back on the ground, his peg leg sliding without much traction, and repeated this action several times. Finally, he was able to position his foot in the lowest notch and grip onto the rock wall with his left hand. Then he struck the rock wall until he had a deep enough notch for his right hand. Alvie placed the eggshell between his teeth, reached his right hand to grip the new notch, and hauled himself up until his left foot was now positioned in the next notch above. His left hand gripped the shell and swung upward to create the next notch. His silver-tooth grin plastered itself across his face.

Two dozen feet into the air, Alvie glanced at the ground below, watching a bead of sweat from his face drip down, down, down.

"Stars. This is high."

But he was so close to the tree branch now. And once he could grip those, he wouldn't be forced to hammer notches while suspended on a rock wall. He shifted the rucksack on his back, wishing he could wipe his brow, and attacked the wall again.

Finally, Alvie's fist wrapped around the tree branch. A chuckle escaped him as he tucked the eggshell into his belt and hauled himself up.

Thirty feet up.

Forty feet up.

Alvie's teeth clenched together until gasps broke free.

His hands screamed as each grip on a new tree branch bit into his palms. His fingers numbed from the cooling afternoon temperature. His arms quivered in fatigue.

"Come on, Alvie!" he shouted, gazing up at his new target. The edge of the cliff was in view now. Only two more tree branches to go!

His arms were like Solstice pudding. "Don't think about that. Think about those lil' turtles."

He hung suspended, the weight of the rucksack twinging his back, willing feeling back into his fingers. He'd catch his breath for one more moment.

Don't think about your arms shaking.

A wrong glance downward made Alvie's heart leap. The ground was so far away. The boulder he'd stood upon appeared as though it were nothing more than an insignificant rock.

Alvie's eyes closed. He inhaled. The scent of his own sweat filled his nose. "Come on, Alvie," he whispered.

His eyes opened and focused on his goal. The next tree branch. That was all he needed to think about right now. Ignoring his trembling, screaming arms, Alvie gulped in a breath and swung himself to the next branch.

He hung limply.

One more.

With energy he was barely able to muster, Alvie reached for the last branch.

Crrraaack!

He'd barely touched it when the branch snapped and tumbled down the wall. Alvie, his weight precariously off-balance, yelped. He threw himself back to the other branch, his hands swiping for anything to grip.

Numb fingers clawed into the branch; it jiggled under his weight. Frantically, his other hand found purchase and seized the tree.

Great exhales echoed in his ears. He heard naught but his heaves of breath and his heart in his chest. Alvie's breaths appeared as great puffs of mist before him, obscuring his sight. His shoulders felt as though they were being stretched from their sockets. His vision grew dizzy.

He hung limply.

As the quaking of the branch slowed, Alvie gazed up to the impossible cliff edge, willing it to come into focus.

Slowly, so slowly, Alvie dared remove one hand from the branch and snatch the half-shell tucked into his belt. He placed it between his teeth and re-gripped the branch, silently praising the goddesses of the moon for having both his hands.

Exhausted was a word that couldn't explain Alvie's fatigue. But there were two choices, one of which entailed Alvie breaking into a thousand pieces.

Come on, Alvie.

Refastening his grip with one hand, Alvie dared remove his other hand, took the shell, swung his foot to give him momentum, and drove the shell into the rock wall. It chipped. Alvie placed the shell back between his teeth, regripped the trembling branch, and then repeated the motion.

He was done counting. He was done singing. He was done smiling. Alvie could do nothing but concentrate on the task, fight his exasperation on how little rock chipped away each time, and strike into the rock wall.

The notch was close to complete when Alvie heard the first *creak* of the branch holding him.

"Siria's skirt."

Another chip into the notch. Another *creak*.

How many more strikes did he have?

Another chip. And the *creak* morphed into a threatening *rrrasssspp*.

With one last strike, Alvie let go of the half-shell, flung his hand back up long enough to get one final grip, swung his torso back, and caught the notch.

Creaaaak.

The branch snapped and fell.

Not one breath of time was wasted. Alvie's other hand reached up, tearing into the cliff's edge. His rucksack did nothing to help with balance or effort.

He calmed his jiggling legs. He needed to lift up his other hand to help himself over the cliff edge. But it was paralyzed in place, clasping the notch.

Come on, Alvie.

'Twas not Alvie's thought, but another's voice in his mind.

"Sloane?" Alvie gasped.

Come on, Alvie.

He didn't question it. There were some things in life one simply did not question. He nodded as if to his friend, hurled his hand up to the edge and with every last piece of strength remaining, hauled himself onto solid ground.

Alvie lay on his back, his chest heaving, his eyes closed.

"Thanks, Sloane," he whispered.

CHAPTER
8

Had Alvie heard Sloane's voice? He decided it did not matter so much now that he had made it to this butte in the mountainside. A cold breeze wrestled past him as he stared down the rock wall, his chest swelling with satisfaction. He drank in the blue of the horizon in the distance, wishing he had someone here to share it with, even Goat.

Yards away, the running stream intersected the dry streambed that had obviously once been a waterfall here. Flipping over, Alvie dragged himself to its bank. After gulping down his fill of water, he watched the stream's movements, hoping that he could take that way down the mountainside on his return journey. Descending the rock wall didn't seem like the best idea.

Where to go now? Would he ever not be surrounded by mountains and rocks again?

What is that?

Standing with a groan, Alvie crossed the stream, wading through the knee-high water. He ignored how, soaked with sweat, it immediately sent a chill through him.

On the opposite bank, mixed with sediment, were small bones. Alvie lifted a small, elongated skull. Stone lizard most likely. He'd certainly seen enough. He tossed it back to the ground, assessing his path. Here on the other side, flanked by more high rock walls, it seemed like another dead end. The only choice was to continue to wade upward through the cool stream.

"Fact o'matter is, there's nothing for it."

He started on his way, moving slowly as his tired muscles protested, determinedly *not* peering down the extreme height of the ridge that appeared along the way.

Up the stream, rounding a curve, Alvie gasped. The mountain opened up, revealing a wide plateau, blue silhouettes of endless mountain peaks along the horizon.

"Goddesses of the moon," Alvie whispered.

The stream continued its meandering path, strewing the banks with foliage like more sagemary bushes, wildflowers, and what looked like river potatoes.

There are worse things to eat.

The landscape of the plateau leading away from the stream was rugged and dry, the coarse ground rust-hued sand and rock. The plateau swept toward a slope. Alvie set down his rucksack and trotted over to inspect it. A massive vein of mountain stone jutted out, creating . . . not a cave exactly, but an overhang of sorts. The bottom, Alvie suspected, was the continuation of the dry streambed.

But something caught his eye.

Scooting on his rear, Alvie skidded down the slope. In the streambed was a hole. Deep. On the other side, the ground was moist, but something ahead clearly blocked the stream.

Alvie lowered himself onto his left knee.

'Twas too odd. It resembled nothing of the other natural phenomena Alvie had encountered in the Monas Territory.

"Not a hole made by mountains."

This hole had been the work of a spade. Mayhap even a few spades. But definitely not natural.

Up and over the slope, Alvie found himself on the other side of the hole, inspecting the cluster of sagemary bushes running along the streambed and against the rock wall.

Why a hole here?

Determining that nothing besides the hole was out of the ordinary, Alvie started back up the slope. Loosened rocks slipped under his peg leg, and he slid into a sagemary bush, his aching muscles screaming as he scrambled to get his firm footing back. He stepped his peg leg out of the bush.

Ting.

That was not rock.

Alvie bent and held the fragment of empty sindri-turtle eggshell in his palm.

"Blimey, another one." But had this one hatched, mayhap? That seemed a possibility. At least, he hoped 'twas a possibility. He marveled at the shimmery shell, tucking it in his belt. Where was the other half of the eggshell? Alvie sat and sifted through the lower branches of the sagemary and sand.

His hand blindly wrapped itself around what felt like the other half of the shell. That is, until he saw it. A complete egg. And 'twas warm. Very warm.

"Ah, lil' baby turtle."

Gingerly, Alvie placed the egg on the ground and dug through the sand with his hands. The grains of sand stung his many cuts, but he continued until he'd unearthed five more eggs.

What had the Cibil said? Sindri turtles laid their eggs where they themselves had hatched and then migrated back to Kage Duna.

Alvie stared into the hole.

Except no turtle could migrate back with a giant hole blocking its path. The pile of rocks that Alvie had come upon days ago suddenly made sense. The migration path of these turtles was being hindered on purpose.

"Good thing there's a hero here."

Alvie reburied the eggs, noting which sagemary bush they nested under, and returned to his rucksack.

Now he had to think. Why would someone want to stop the sindri turtles?

He withdrew the eggshell from his belt. Certainly, these shells might be worth something. Also, the beautiful shells of the turtles could fetch the price. He envisioned the exquisite turquoise shells etched with unique swirling designs. And what of the seemingly magical qualities of the sindris? They'd turned a sludgy swamp into a crystal-clear lake. Was there something more than simply eating the algae?

"Who are you?" a gruff voice behind Alvie asked.

Alvie turned, his heart racing in surprise, to face three people in a line. First, stood a large man with slicked back long hair and a nose ring. Beside him, was a woman with mean eyes, which were accentuated by a deep scar running across one eyebrow. She wore a necklace of rocks beaded like a high-born woman might wear a string a Mehr Sea pearls. The other man was not much taller than Alvie and with a great stomach protruding from his tunic. A grey beard over a wrinkly face clearly showed him as the oldest of the three.

They stared at the turtle eggshell in Alvie's hand.

"Hallo!" Alvie waved, dropping the hand that held the shell to his side. "Lovely afternoon, ain't it?"

"Where did you get that eggshell?" the woman asked.

"Eggshell?"

"The eggshell in your hand."

"Oh." Alvie held it up in the late afternoon sunlight. "That what this is? I thought it was some kind of rock, you know. Certainly are a lot of rocks 'round here."

The three moved toward him. "Give it to me," spoke the pot-bellied man.

"Course." Alvie dropped the half-shell into his hand. "What kind of shell is that?"

The large man and the woman sniggered while the older man held the half-shell to eye level. "Turtle. You found any more?" he asked.

"Nah. Just this one. And that was way back there." Alvie made a grand gesture with both arms. "I mean, way, way back there."

The old man nodded, placing the half-shell in a satchel slung over his shoulder. "What are you doing here?"

"Just explorin'. I'm a mapmaker, you know. For the Baron of Gran."

"That right?"

"Aye. Just came from Clemen. You been up here long? In Monas, I mean?"

"That's our affair."

"Course. Didn't mean nothin' by that. Just been a long time since I talked to anyone."

"You certain you haven't seen more of these shells?" the large man asked, folding his arms at his chest.

Alvie didn't blink. "Nah. I'm pretty sure I'd remember something like that. I've—"

"If you're a mapmaker, where are your sketch items?" the woman asked.

"Aye, Steff is right," the large man said. "Where *are* your sketch items?"

"Ah, you wouldn't believe it if I told you."

"Try us."

"Would love to. 'Tis a great story. You have a camp? A fire? Fact o'matter is, we all know once that sun goes over the mountains"— he thumbed toward the sinking sun— "it gets right difficult to see or be warm. If you have a cookfire, I can make us some river potatoes like you ain't ne'er had." He slid his rucksack off one shoulder—the action causing the three to stiffen—and dug through it until he found the tiny pouch of salt.

"What is that?"

"What's that? Stars, don't tell me you've ne'er had salt before."

"Salt?" Steff's eyes widened. "'Tis been an age since we had anything flavored, Mett."

"Watch it," Mett, the old man, chided. His hardened expression surveyed Alvie up and down as he rested his hands on his paunch. "I'm not interested in stories. You have news from Clemen? Six moons have passed since we've left these mountains."

"News? Aye. Brace yourself. You've missed a lot."

The large man shrugged. "I could eat some river potatoes."

"Very well," Mett said. "This way. What did you say your name was?"

"Alvie."

The three backtracked along the stream, Alvie stomping wearily along after.

Alvie the hero. He bore determined eyes into their backs.

CHAPTER
9

Good storytelling was a dose of the truth mixed with colorful elaboration. Mett may have professed to not be interested in stories, but by the time Alvie was finished with his tale of the Battle for the Unsung, a monster story about defeating the Befallen, Mett sat just as wide-eyed as Steff and the large man, whose name Alvie learned was Trauts. Alvie had omitted his own role in the tale, which certainly wasn't the full truth—but Alvie knew that sometimes reality could seem too untrue to be believed. He knew the proper amount of truth to insert. 'Twas how all good stories were after all.

Following a few warm-up stories he always told strangers about his dabbling in various trades—everything from a scribe's assistant to a lute tuner—the others readily seemed to accept him as a mapmaker who had dropped his materials and painfully witnessed them flow downstream and out of sight into a cave. The existence of the cave was factual, and Alvie felt certain they'd be familiar enough with the landscape here, including the cave the stream led into, to believe him. The right dose of truth.

He trusted these three like he trusted walking barefoot in a meadow full of field eels. He'd hoped that his open use of storytelling, a currency that had opened many doors to Alvie, would encourage them to spout a few stories in kind. Unfortunately, if Trauts and Steff had wanted to share anything, Mett quickly shut them up.

But Alvie could see with this last story about the Befallen's defeat, Mett began to soften.

"My, my, but that is some tale, Alvie," Steff said, taking a last bite of the river potatoes.

"Aye. Almost wouldn't believe it if I hadn't seen it for myself. Told you that you'd missed a lot." Alvie discarded his tin plate next to him, wondering how many more river potatoes he could have eaten.

Mett nodded, his focus on the fire they sat around. "Well, 'tis comforting to know that the Befallen is gone for good. And the way you described those knights—the Wolf, those from the Order of Siria—'tis almost like you personally know them."

"Just a good observer, I s'pose," Alvie said, not missing a beat.

"I suppose that's why the baron employed you as a mapmaker."

Alvie shrugged. "Could be."

A small *squeak* probed its way into the night. Alvie's neck rotated toward the sound. The others either did not hear it or remained unconcerned.

A few moments later, Trauts stood and said he needed to check on something. The other two paid him no heed.

The *squeak* sounded again, but this time, Alvie kept his head still.

"So, you three been up here for a long while. Did you celebrate the Solstice Moon? That's one of my favorites. I'm a gourmet when it comes to solstice stew. You like solstice stew?"

Mett's eyes darted to where Trauts had disappeared. Without a word, he stood and walked away.

Alvie watched Steff to gauge the legitimacy of the unease prickling through him. He was unready to fight or flee with his body so weary from the climb up the cliff earlier.

"I like solstice stew well enough," Steff said, making Alvie's body tense from her abrupt, late response.

"Aye? Fact o' matter, I make a mean solstice stew."

"I wager you do," Steff said, running her index finger along her empty plate to wipe up the remnants of salt before sticking it in her mouth. "I've eaten many river potatoes, and none as good as those."

"My thanks," Alvie said.

A pause followed.

"So, 'bout those turtle shells you was askin' after earlier," Alvie kept his voice casual, "what you want with those? They valuable or something?"

"I hear they can be," Steff said, absentmindedly fidgeting with her rock necklace. Not exactly a confession. "But 'tis poaching." Her eyes lifted to his; her gaze was piercing. Waiting.

"Poaching, you say? That seems ridiculous. Who cares about a few turtles?"

Steff's shoulders relaxed and she went on. "I hear, though, that a few years ago since the sovereign was so consumed with the Befallen, it has become easier for poachers to earn a little coin. There are traders, mostly from Vathnava, who will pay a hefty price for sindri turtles or their eggshells."

"That so?" Alvie asked, giving a casual frown.

"Aye. A half-shell like the one you handed over . . . well, you might not be pleased to know how much you might have fetched for it. Mayhap a sack of gold?"

Alvie coughed.

"Mayhap not." Steff's eyes narrowed. "That shell was not the best quality. But a whole turtle shell might even be enough to repurch—" Steff turned red and spluttered, "Er, acquire some land."

"Times have been so desperate, a person's got to do what they can to earn their keep. That's what I say, anyway," Alvie said, shrugging.

Steff gave a genuine smile. "That's what I say, also. Hard times, these."

Alvie's heartbeat thumped in his ears.

"Mayhap you'd like to make a little coin?" Steff asked.

"I ne'er turn that opportunity down." Alvie barked out a laugh.

Steff hung her head as if in thought. When she met Alvie's eyes again, she had an expression of desperation. "Only thing is, the trail of sindri turtles seems to have dried up. You certain you haven't seen any more eggshells like the one you were holding when we ran into you? I mean, 'twas only half of a shell."

Alvie thought of the warm, heavy eggs under the sagemary bushes, and did not even blink as he replied, "Nah. Definitely not."

Steff stood, her gaze darkening. "That is unfortunate. Because we have no use for you if we cannot trust you."

Coming out of the shadows were Trauts and Mett. Trauts held Alvie's rucksack. Mett held half of a turtle eggshell.

Alvie's stomach dropped. *The shell from the cliff.* He had forgotten about the eggshell tucked in his rucksack.

"You certain you cannot remember where you found this?" Mett asked, holding up the shell. The firelight smeared deep shadows on his face. "You said earlier that you were a great observer."

Alvie stood, silently cursing when his exhausted legs wobbled, and steeled himself. "True. But I've also been known to forget things."

Trauts lunged toward him.

WHEN ALVIE GAINED CONSCIOUSNESS, HE FOUND THAT HIS arms were bound tightly behind his back, and he sat against a giant rock.

One eye refused to open, his nose leaked blood into his mouth, and his jaw ached. Not to mention his temples and neck. He could not decide what hurt the most. *All* his head hurt. This was a headache unlike any he'd had before. Trauts had not gone easy on him. His stump had been saved in the beating, but carefully shifting his throbbing body and squinting in the morning sunlight, Alvie felt a flash of hot pain in the amputated limb. It had been some time since he'd had to endure having his peg leg strapped to his thigh all night.

For a moment, Alvie worried that his captors had simply tied him up and fled, leaving him to face a slow terrible death, but then someone cleared his throat, making Alvie flinch. Trauts stood nearby holding a waterskin. Alvie winced again, ready for more pounding, but the big man stepped toward him and held the waterskin to Alvie's lips.

Alvie drank with vigor, water dribbling down his sore chin, then gasped, "Thank you!"

"They shall return soon. You must tell them where you found those eggshells. Mett would sooner kill you, but I convinced him that you would see reason this morning and tell him."

"And what if I did know and did tell him?" Alvie asked. He worked his jaw side to side. "You three gonna leave me alive?"

Squeak.

Trauts stepped away and when he returned, he carried a baby sindri turtle. It fit in the palm of his hand; its petite legs were smaller than Trauts's fingers. It craned its neck, surveying its surroundings, its huge black eyes shining. It let out another squeak.

Alvie couldn't help but coo.

What could he say to escape this situation?

"How can you poach these lil' fellas? Is the price so great that you'd risk being caught? Besides, do you *want* to stay up here? This place ain't naught but rocks!"

When Trauts didn't meet Alvie's eye, he knew he'd sparked something in the giant man—whether it be conscience or plain weariness, he didn't know, but mayhap Alvie could build a story that Trauts could become attached to.

"The truth is there are plenty of ways to make an honest livin'. And you're big and strong. Why not enlist for the new sovereign? Or become a cobbler? If you like shoes, that is. Or, you could be a . . . a sailor! Sounds as if you're already familiar with North Port, from what Steff mentioned last night. Just—"

"North Port has changed in the last five years. I'm already . . . known there."

Alvie nodded in understanding. "Well, there's always the port of Kestriel."

"I worked in the cinth mines, a long time ago. Before the mines dried up."

"Did you like it?"

Trauts nodded.

"Well then, they have cinth mines in the Capella Realm, don't they?"

Trauts shrugged. "I've never been off the island."

"Me either, but it cannot be called the Empire of Light for no good reason, can it?

Trauts placed the sindri turtle on the ground. It began exploring in tiny, tiny steps. Trauts's gaze softened as he observed it. Finally, he said, "I cannot. I cannot leave Steff." His voice quieted. "And I am bound to Mett. I owe him a debt."

Stars. Alvie knew about owing debts. "Look, untie me and we'll leave together. We can save them lil' sindri turtle eggs. Take them down the mountain and—"

"Interesting what you can hear when you do not make your presence known right away," Mett's voice came. Alvie's shoulders tightened. "I knew he'd yammer. That blabbermouth is ripe to say anything,"

Trauts averted his gaze from Alvie.

Mett and Steff came to tower over Alvie on the ground. Mett's foot hovered above the baby turtle, which had crawled close to Alvie. "What eggs and where are they?"

"Ah, I don't know."

"I can break this baby turtle here before your eyes or I can have Trauts break *you* some more."

Alvie couldn't risk harm to the tiny turtle. But Mett wouldn't hurt the baby turtle, would he? 'Twas too valuable. The Night Caller must have had some tight spots he'd escaped from. Same with Sir Tolvar. Alvie would do the same. He just needed some time. "I don't know what you're talking about."

"Trauts, break his nose."

Alvie sighed and braced himself as, without the least bit of hesitation, a giant fist collided with his face. His head slammed back into the rock and all Alvie saw was white, hot pain.

"Wait!" Alvie said, spitting blood. "Wait!"

Think, Alvie.

Trauts fist plowed into him again. Alvie's nose went *crack.*

"All right! All right! I'll show you. 'Tis over by where the river potatoes were growing."

Mett's foot shadowed the baby turtle once more. "I am not in the habit of entertaining myself with others' stupidity."

"I am telling you! They are over by the river. I'll show you." Alvie ran his tongue over his teeth to make sure they were all still intact.

"Well then, let us pack up camp and go find them." Mett lifted the baby turtle in his palm. "And let's hope for everyone's sake that you're correct."

HOURS LATER, AT THE RIVERBANKS, ALVIE LOOKED ON in secret amusement as Steff and Trauts dug their fifth hole. He'd been surprised that Mett had not forced Alvie into digging alongside them, but after he'd nodded at the ground beneath the sagemary bushes, they'd simply thrown Alvie, still bound, to the ground. The bitter smell of sagemary filled the air as dug-up bushes piled higher and higher in a heap near the holes.

"I can't explain why they aren't there," Alvie said after regarding Mett's angry expression. "Like I said, they were buried under them bushes."

Steff let out an impressive stream of profanities as their latest hole failed to reveal any eggs.

Trauts wiped his brow, leaning on his spade. "Do you need a rest?" he asked Steff.

She snorted. "I'm fine. Let's toss him around some more." Steff threw her spade onto the ground.

Trauts nodded and lifted Alvie by his collar. "Where are they?"

"Stars. How should I know? This is where you spotted me, isn't it? Do sindris have any predators? I mean, besides fools who want to go wipin' them out for no reason?"

"I need them!" Steff shouted.

Mett climb out of the hole, his expression dark. "Tell us where they are!"

Alvie gave Mett a pointed look with his good eye, the other tender and half-closed from his black eye. "What did I say before we came? By the river and under sagemary bushes. You think I want to keep being punched around?"

Trauts dropped Alvie to the ground. He let out a groan.

"He must be lying," Steff said.

"But what about predators, eh?" Alvie struggled to sit. "I seen plenty of stone lizards 'round here. I s'pose you have, too, at least once and awhile. Don't stone lizards eat eggs?"

The three shared a look. Alvie knew he was close. "Fact o'matter is, I saw lizard bones down that trail." He nodded toward the trail that had first led him here. "If they sensed food up here, 'course they'd come this way."

"They would drag them to their den," Steff muttered. "Remember that time—"

"Shut it, woman," Mett silenced her.

"There's no need for that." Trauts grimaced at Mett. "She's trying to be helpful."

"Enough!" Mett shouted. He eyed his comrades then said to Steff, "You stay here. Trauts and I will investigate."

Alvie watched their retreating backs until they were around the bend and out of sight. Steff, too, watched, scowling at the back of Mett's head and toying with the rock necklace, muttering to herself. Alvie couldn't catch everything she said, but he thought he heard, "Soon. Not much more." She resumed prodding the holes with her spade.

It was only then that Alvie dared glance at the sagemary bushes near the overhang where six little turtle eggs remained buried.

CHAPTER
10

Mayhap if Alvie had not had a third roughing up, he could have fallen asleep that night. But upon Mett and Trauts's return, dripping wet from the waist down, Trauts holding the same skull Alvie had discovered, but otherwise empty handed, Mett had ordered Alvie be beaten anew.

Trauts gave only the slightest hesitation before Steff asked him what he was waiting for.

They'd resumed digging into the night, and after dark, rather than trek back to where they had stationed their camp, it was decided they'd sleep here.

Mett had taken the first watch over Alvie and had spent the entire time threatening Alvie or the baby turtle he held or both. Neither Steff nor Trauts had slept much—Alvie glimpsed every now and again their bug-eyed glares at their leader. Trauts's watch had begun quiet, but Alvie let questions trickle out—slowly at first—questions like where was Trauts born? Why did he like working in the cinth mines so much? What did he plan on doing once this sindri turtle poaching expedition was over? After all, there were only so many turtles left, probably. Did he miss ale and pub fare? How did he meet Mett and Steff? Did he find their company agreeable?

All the while, Alvie kept glancing at Mett and Steff to assess their slumber. Mett had chosen to hunker down yards away from them behind a large boulder and Alvie couldn't tell if he slept or not. But Steff. The whites of her eyes drilling angrily into Alvie were evident in the light from the crackling campfire.

The baby turtle nestled in its crate, unmoving.

Trauts had not answered any of Alvie's questions, but his mouth plunged into a firm line and his shoulders rounded as he stared at nothing.

"All right, if you don't want to answer any questions, maybe you'd like a right good story."

"Nay!" Trauts stood and scrubbed his hand over his face. "Enough! You better tell Mett where those eggs are in the morning, or he'll order me to—listen! You must tell him."

"All right. No story. You got a sweetheart somewhere? Your eye on anyone?"

"Cease!" Trauts leapt up and moved to where Steff lay. Judging by her uneven chest movement, she'd finally fallen asleep.

He shook her shoulder gingerly. "Steff. 'Tis your watch. I cannot take any more of this."

Steff picked up a handful of sand and threw it into Trauts's face. He shouted in anger as his hands flew to his eyes and he instinctively kicked, landing his foot into her side. She hollered.

"Stars, Steff! I'm sorry. I did not mean to—"

"What in Siria's skirt is going on?" Mett's voice suddenly shook the air.

"He kicked me!" Steff yelled.

"'Twas an accident! You flung sand into my eye!"

"Goddesses of the moon, cease this!" Mett stood. His scowl landed on Alvie. "You. As I said earlier, you have until the morning to decide. 'Tis the eggs or you!" Mett grabbed his bed roll and turned to the others. "And you two. Keep shut. I've had enough. If anyone wakes me up again, 'tis your head!" He marched away.

"My thanks, Trauts." Steff jerked her head in the direction of Mett before muttering, "I cannot wait to be away from here."

Trauts tossed Steff an injured glance she did not notice, and he too moved his bed roll, to the far side of the campfire.

Alvie shrugged at Steff as she stood and stretched. She sleepily rubbed her eyes and leaned against a boulder. She withdrew a knife from her pocket, unsheathed it, and waved it in Alvie's direction. "Do not dare say one word."

Alvie clamped his lips together and winked. Steff's murmur of frustration bounced off the rock walls.

"I mean it!" Mett shouted from the distance.

Steff's cheeks bloomed in contrast to her scowl.

"Good night then," Alvie whispered and closed his eyes.

And waited.

So as to not fall asleep, and to distract himself from how his entire body ached, Alvie silently told himself every folktale he could think of. Ancient tales. Some about the goddesses of the moon. The Rainless Moon goddess, who sacrificed herself to end a seven-year drought. The Hoarfrost Moon goddess, a milkmaid turned warrior who trapped the banshees in the Cave of the Shapeless Memories. And Alvie's favorite, the Hunger Moon goddess, a beggar who thanked hospitable strangers with a basket of bread that never ran out.

Alvie's stomach growled.

He winked an eye open. Steff's breathing had fallen into a rhythmic pattern a couple of stories ago. An hour's half earlier, she had finally slumped to the ground. Through cracked eyelids, keeping his own breathing as heavy as possible, Alvie had watched her strain to keep her own eyes open for several minutes. She'd moved restlessly, tossing her knife from one hand to the other, rubbing her hands together, stoking the campfire halfheartedly, craning her neck and back into a stretch, before finally tugging her cloak tighter around herself against night's chill and surrendering to slumber, evident in her relaxed shoulders.

Studying her with caution, Alvie slowly sat up. Low snoring exuded from Trauts. Mett was too far away to hear similar sounds from him, but Alvie could not discern any movement from his direction.

The campfire had sighed into embers, the stream purling nearby.

Every movement was one of deliberation, and Alvie's eyes never left Steff, who gave a small snort in her sleep. After a few attempts to stand, his limbs numb from the cold and staying in one position too long, Alvie carefully crossed over to the crate of the baby turtle, gingerly placing his peg leg with every step. The door of the crate was mercly latched, not locked. The baby turtle stared at Alvie with its large, glossy onyx eyes. Thinking better of simply unlatching the door while his hands were still bound behind him, Alvie conceded that he needed Steff's knife.

Slow paces brought Alvie next to Steff. The knife lay discarded next to her.

Alvie steadied his breath, fixed on Steff's sleeping form.

Turning around, Alvie knelt on his left knee, shifted backwards, and searched for the knife behind him. His fingers grazed the cold steel of the blade and clasped around the worn wooden handle.

Got it.

Taking as much time as his thighs would allow, Alvie came

out of his kneeling position. He wobbled on his peg leg and nearly toppled into Steff.

An involuntary grunt escaped him, and the knife almost dropped from his hand as he righted himself and held his breath waiting for Steff to awaken.

Alvie waited.

And waited.

He glanced at Trauts, still snoring as if to rival a bear.

Nothing.

When Alvie was next to the turtle crate again, he felt safer about sawing his bindings. Methodically, stopping every now and then to survey everyone's sleeping forms, Alvie finally sliced through the rope. He pocketed the knife, massaged his sore wrists, then wiped sweat from his brow.

Alvie needed his rucksack. He could not carry six turtle eggs and a baby turtle in his arms all the way down the mountain.

Squeak!

"Shhh!" Alvie's palms flew into the air. "Shhh."

The baby turtle blinked at him but did not squeak again.

Where is that rucksack? He scanned over the area, hoping to spot it.

He would have to search for it.

He'd taken two silent steps when, *Squeak!*

The baby turtle leaned against the door, its small neck craning between two bars.

Alvie doubled back. "Shhh. You must stay quiet," he whispered. Frantically, he glanced at Steff's face, dimly visible in the dark.

Please still be asleep.

Nothing about her appearance had changed. Thank the stars for Trauts's snoring.

Every moment that Alvie stood here was an opportunity for everyone to awake. And that would not be good. He had to move.

Deciding that releasing the baby turtle might help it to be quiet, Alvie opened the crate and placed the little critter on the ground. It stared up at him, as if questioning what it was supposed to do. Well, he'd fetch it in a moment. With a bit more haste, Alvie skulked around the camp, scanning for the rucksack.

About to give up his search, he glimpsed it mere feet from Mett, next to the nearest hole.

That about makes sense.

Alvie crept toward the rucksack, careful to not clink his peg leg against the rock. From here, he could make out Mett's sleeping form. A dagger lay next to him.

That wouldn't be the worst thing to take along.

Alvie inched toward the dagger.

Abruptly, Mett moaned. His eyelids fluttered. Alvie stumbled and caught himself just in time to stop himself from tripping into the hole. He froze. Mett shifted onto his side away from Alvie, tugging his blanket over his shoulder.

Alvie snatched up the dagger and the rucksack and padded toward the turtle. He scooped it up as he moved. He'd waste no more time! He made it to the stream. All he had to do was cross, quickly dig up the eggs, and then wade down the stream away from here. He could be at the stream junction before it was light out.

Squeak!

"Cease!" Mett's voice came from behind.

Alvie went rigid, heart pounding in his ears. Then—

"Wake up! Get up!" Mett shouted.

Stars almighty. I was so close.

Alvie turned around; Mett bolted toward him.

Without a second thought, Alvie tossed the baby turtle into the stream. It floated down the current into the darkness.

"Ahhh!" Mett cried, rushing toward the stream. "Get that turtle!"

By now, Trauts and Steff were on their feet. Trauts stumbled toward them, still half-asleep.

Alvie pointed the old man's dagger at his chest when he was a few feet away. "That's it! I'm leaving now, and you can just stay put."

Trauts barked out a laugh, coming to stand next to Mett.

Steff whirled around, searching the ground. "Where is my knife?"

Alvie gave a half-smile.

"Enough!" Mett said, although he did not make a move toward the outstretched dagger. "Steff, after that turtle! 'Tis all we have!"

Throwing up her arms, a groan shot out of her mouth. She ran past Alvie and burst into the stream. In the darkness, 'twas impossible to see how far the baby turtle had traveled. Alvie prayed it'd already flowed downstream.

Steff's steps kicked up splashes of frigid water as she chased after the vanished baby turtle and disappeared around the bend. Alvie threw her a quick glance before resuming his focus on the others.

"Give me that dagger, boy. You don't even know what to do with it," Mett said.

"You right certain 'bout that?" Alvie said, changing his stance so his weight was on his left foot. His body felt hot all over as his pulse quickened in anticipation of a fight. He took a quick step forward and swiped the dagger at Mett just as Ghlee had taught him. A gash in Mett's tunic, just under his shoulder, appeared in the moonlight. For a moment, everyone—Alvie included—gawked in surprise.

"I mean it," Alvie said, recovering and raising his chin. "Don't come any further."

"Enough," Mett said, inspecting his wound through the collar of his tunic. "Get him."

Trauts glanced in the direction Steff had gone before he obeyed, moving toward Alvie.

A scream, shrill and chilling, leapt out of the distance.

All three turned in the direction it'd come. Ice slid over Alvie's spine.

Steff.

The scream curdled in his ears a second time.

"Steff!" Trauts stepped toward the stream. Alvie took a step to follow him.

Mett broke his focus from down the stream. "Where are you going?"

"To help her!"

"She doesn't need help. She's fine!" Mett straightened. "Get him. We need those eggs so we can collect that coin!"

Trauts paused.

"Are you really not going to help her?" Alvie gazed up at Trauts. "That sounds real bad."

"Mett!" Trauts shouted. He'd already taken two steps away from Alvie, one foot already in the stream.

A third scream. This time cut short.

Stars.

"The turtle!" Mett exclaimed and dashed into the stream.

"You mean Steff!" Alvie called after him.

"Take care of him! When we sell those eggs, we'll be square!" Mett yelled as he vanished into the night.

Trauts hesitated.

"Go help her!"

Trauts shuffled his feet, gaze distant.

"Trauts, seriously."

The big man stooped.

"Seriously," Alvie repeated. "What is more valuable?"

Trauts clenched his jaw and launched himself at Alvie.

Taken by surprise, Alvie nearly dropped the dagger, which he'd been holding loosely at his side. But in the nick of time, he swung the dagger at the bigger man, heartened when he grazed Trauts. But a slash to the upper arm wasn't too much to celebrate; Trauts leapt at Alvie again, swinging his fists. He sidestepped and swung the dagger again, hitting nothing but air. After more dodging and ducking on the part of both men, Alvie's breath was labored. He was out of moves. Trauts seemed to be toying with him. The bigger man snickered.

"Aaarghhh!" Alvie yelled, lunging at Trauts and taking him off balance.

Alvie landed on top of him and hovered the dagger over Trauts's chest. "Surrender?"

Trauts said nothing and swung a meaty arm, knocking the dagger out of Alvie's hand. It *clanged* to the ground. Before he could reach for it, Alvie took a punch to the cheek. Angry now, blinded by pain, Alvie threw his own fist in the direction of Trauts's face and, surprisingly, the man cried out as a *crack* rang through the air. Alvie's fist throbbed. He smashed his other fist down against Trauts's nose.

"Ooph."

Trauts raised his fists, but Alvie slammed his fist into him again, ignoring the pulsing in his fists.

With one last uppercut to the jaw, Trauts's eyes rolled and then closed.

Alvie spit blood, still sitting atop Trauts's chest. "No one ever thinks I got strength."

He stood, glancing at Trauts's unconscious form before extending his fingers in pain. The skin over his knuckles was split, his fingers swelling. But he couldn't concern himself with that now.

Alvie sprang into action. Grabbing the rucksack, he splashed across the stream, half-ran, half-slid down the slope and began digging into the sand as fast as he could.

No eggs. His blood ran cold. Did they—

But nay, they didn't have the eggs.

He dug more frantically, sand flying into his face. He stopped, brushing sand off his nose and wincing from the pain the movement caused.

This is the wrong sagemary bush.

"Blast!"

He stood and tried to gauge which bush it was. The moonlight was no help at all. Alvie desperately selected a different bush at random and began digging. He cracked a silver-toothed grin when his fingers wrapped around the oblong shape of the first turtle egg. One into the rucksack. Two. Three. In the rucksack. Within seconds, Alvie had scooped up the other three eggs and tucked all six inside. He patted it and raced back up the slope, ignoring how his every muscle ached.

At the top, he glanced to where he'd left Trauts sprawled out on the ground.

He was gone.

"Stars," Alvie whispered. He scanned the area, taking Steff's knife out of his pocket.

Footsteps behind made him whirl, but Trauts's fist had already landed its first punch when Alvie met his gaze. Alvie slammed into the ground, the knife hurling away well out of reach.

Trauts held Mett's dagger over him.

That would have been a good thing to remember to grab.

CHAPTER
11

For the second time, Alvie awoke with his hands tightly secured behind his back. This time, his thighs were also bound. It was not quite dawn, but not quite night either. At first, Alvie thought—nay, hoped—he'd stumbled into a new nightmare and mayhap he was not quite awake. But he knew he was. He was too hungry, too sore, and too tired to not be.

Trauts was gone.

Probably went to help Steff and Mett.

Alvie tugged against the ropes. The moment the poachers returned, he might as well be praying to the stars for forgiveness for all his wrongdoings. He was as good as dead. Escaping these bindings was all that mattered.

Pulling, twisting, jerking, it didn't matter. Trauts had knotted the bindings as tight as they could be.

"So much for my hero's title," Alvie whispered.

He'd failed. He'd never be a knight like Sir Tolvar. Or a hero like Sloane. Or a warrior like the Night Caller.

The ropes became an enemy he thirsted to conquer and with renewed determination, Alvie wrestled with the bindings. But though he tried, 'twas to no avail. Heave. Nothing. Yank. Nothing.

Alvie panted, his chin resting on his chest. All he'd desired was to help the Cibil and those little turtles. Nothing was certain, but

Alvie was sure that other than those eggs, there were likely only a few sindri turtles left on the continent.

On the continent!

And now they'd disappear into extinction forever. The Cibil would lose his home. The world would lose the Cibil. All because Alvie hadn't even been able to best three lowlife poachers.

He'd failed.

The rucksack rested near the now-dead campfire. Taunting Alvie.

Despite himself, Alvie began to shiver. They'd be back any moment. What was he going to do? How would he get out of this?

He fought the bindings again, the coarse rope cutting into his wrists. Behind his knees, the friction of the twisting rope made the leather strap of his peg leg chafe his hamstring.

A small whimper escaped him. Immediately, Alvie pursed his lips together, reddening. His shoulders slumped, and he allowed the babble of the stream distract him.

He truly had failed.

From behind him, a scuffing of steps on rock caught Alvie's breath in his throat. 'Twas all over now. His eyelids clenched shut.

A chatter followed.

Alvie's eyes popped open; his breath held.

Chatter chatter.

Slowly, Alvie craned his neck. Nothing.

He turned back; there it was. He was face to face with the hoshefer.

It stood on its hind legs, its enormous bushy tail wagging back and forth. It rotated its head from side to side, wrinkling its tiny pink nose. Then it chattered again as if the two were already engaged in a casual conversation.

"Am I glad to see you," Alvie said.

It went on all fours and crawled *onto* Alvie. It leaned forward, its little teeth tattling together rapidly as it sniffed Alvie's chest.

He could do naught but freeze.

Again, it rose onto its hind legs before pivoting to sniff the bindings at Alvie's legs.

"Aye. I'm stuck. Can you help?"

Absurd. This was absurd.

Suddenly, the hoshefer bolted away and disappeared behind a rock.

"Wait!" He heard no other sound and prayed that the hoshefer had not detected the others returning.

But in a moment, it returned, this time from a different direction. It stalked on all fours toward Alvie, but stepped in a cautious manner, every so often halting. Then it sped toward him—Alvie gave a shout of surprise—and ducked itself behind him. Alvie waited. The hoshefer stood motionless.

Could it chew through the bindings?

The hoshefer gave a soft chomp on the rope, its whiskers creating a slight tickle against Alvie's skin.

Holy stars! I'm saved.

Abruptly, it ceased.

He waited for it to resume its chomping, but nothing happened. It crept next to him, sniffing along his torso. It stopped when it came to the rope around his thighs, curiously scrutinizing his peg leg.

Alvie held his breath. Mayhap it would chew through the rope around his thighs.

Instead, the hoshefer wrinkled its nose and then gnawed on his peg leg.

"Oi!" Alvie jerked away. "Stop that!"

The hoshefer stood on it hind legs and moved its teeth to his peg leg again.

Alvie jerked the peg leg away again. "I mean it!"

Chatter chatter. The hoshefer seemed to shrug as it wobbled between its hind legs and tail and then darted out of sight.

"Well, my thanks for that!" Alvie shouted.

His eyes drew to the tiny teeth marks on his peg leg. Stars, how his stump ached from so many days in a row of not being able to remove it.

Remove it.

Alvie righted himself from his slumped position as best he could. Aye, remove it. If he could somehow remove his peg leg, he could get his legs out of their bindings. And then . . . could he wiggle his bound arms around his rear so they were in front of him? Mayhap Alvie could unknot the rope with his teeth.

"Fact o'matter is, there's nothing for it."

But how to slip off his peg leg when it was strapped tightly against his thigh? Could he pull it off somehow? Pulling against the rope had twisted the strap. Mayhap it wasn't so tight.

How much time did Alvie have?

Scooting on his rear, Alvie wedged his peg leg against a boulder, braced the weight of his left foot against it, and placing his bound palms on the ground for leverage, tugged against the strap of the peg leg. The strap bit into his thigh. Tears formed at the crease of his eyes. When he couldn't muster the same pressure any longer, Alvie dropped onto his rear and concentrated on his raw palms so the agony of his stump didn't overwhelm him.

He panted. The strap had not budged. Spotty, invisible stars danced before him. The prickling of phantom pain burned.

"Come on, Alvie."

With a deep breath, Alvie braced his peg leg and pushed his weight in opposition of the strap. He let out a groan as he felt the twist of strap give way slightly. He let himself take another quick break. Despite the chill of the early hour, sweat beaded at his forehead and neck.

The hoshefer appeared. It chattered.

"I don't think I can do it."

Chatter.

Alvie took that as encouragement. Gritting his teeth, he tried again. This time, the strap slipped more than an inch onto the back of his kneecap.

"One more ought to do it."

But stars, it hurt. Alvie slumped, unable to decide what part of his body hurt most.

Chatter chatter.

With a huff, Alvie exerted himself again. He pulled against the peg leg. His left leg screamed from forcing itself against it. Slowly, slowly, the strap gave and shifted.

One more heave and all at once Alvie's stump slipped out of the strap and free of the peg leg.

The peg leg dropped to the ground.

For the next few minutes, Alvie simply collected his breath and winced through the incredible pain.

Now he had to wriggle his stump out of the rope. The rope had loosened ever so slightly, but that didn't mean that it wouldn't be a task. Alvie spent the next few minutes, flexing his stump against the rope, begging muscles that were not nearly as strong as the rest of him to bend and tug and pull, until, out of breath and sweat dripping from his forehead, his right kneecap escaped the rope.

But he wasn't finished. And his stump stung like it'd been freshly amputated.

For a moment, Alvie wondered if he might pass out. He kept his focus on the babble of the water while he waited for the moment that the others would return.

The hoshefer had disappeared. That couldn't be good.

"Fact o'matter, ye got to keep goin'."

The next step felt like a piece of Harvest pie comparatively. Alvie made use of his slender build. He wiggled his bound hands underneath him, stretching his long arms 'til his shoulders burned. Then they were past his rear, and from there he could easily slide them up around his legs, over his stump. In no time, he'd worked his other leg out of the circle of his arms and had the rope binding his wrists at eye-level.

Still. Even that easier step hadn't been easy. Alvie wanted to flop down and give in to exhaustion. But his time was running out.

Grasping the middle of the knot between his teeth, Alvie wrenched the rope. He figured it would take three tries.

It took eight.

Finally, the rope slithered off his wrists. Alvie rubbed where they were most sore before moving to his jaw and massaging that, too. His jaw *already* throbbed from Trauts's fists.

Absentmindedly, Alvie removed the loose rope from his leg before rolling up the leg of his hose to examine his stump.

New raw notches blotched above his kneecap where he'd worked so hard to pull the strap of the peg leg off.

And now he had to put his peg leg back on.

His eye caught the returned hoshefer observing him on a nearby rock in the looming sunrise. The first blue light of dawn settled over the rocks.

It could be any moment now.

Alvie's fingers wrapped around the peg leg. But then he set it down. Instead, he tore at the bottom of his hose and carefully wrapped the cloth around his kneecap and thigh. There was nothing for it. He strapped on the peg leg over the cloth, ignoring the fact that it did little to help the pain.

Still, Alvie couldn't help the half-smile that slid across his lips. Now that would be a story to tell, how having a removable leg had saved him.

He stood, stumbled to his rucksack, and gathered it up in only a few heartbeats. Next to it was Steff's knife. Alvie plucked it from the ground and placed it in his pocket.

"That was a right good idea, lil' fella," Alvie said. He scanned the area, but the hoshefer was gone.

Well, he couldn't waste time even if he would like the hoshefer's company. But how to leave? Surely, they would return via the stream. He couldn't go that way if he hoped to never meet them again. There was little other option. Go further up the mountain? That would probably entail scaling another tall rock wall. The sunrise was in full swing now. He had to think of something. Eyeing where the eggs had been buried across the stream under the sagemary bushes, Alvie considered the hole under the overhang in the empty streambed that had been created to keep the turtles from trekking that way. Would that he had time to fill it.

The two spades lay carelessly discarded next to the holes that had been dug yesterday.

Alvie fetched one and went to stand in the dried streambed under the overhang. Aye, much too deep to fill in. Mayhap he could tiptoe past the hole, and journey down this old streambed to the intersection of the streams down the mountain? It'd take a risk. There was nothing guaranteed about that direction.

I got to try.

Just then, a loud *splosh* met his ears. It could only be the approach of the poachers.

Goddesses of the moon!

Alvie hugged his back to the rock wall, frantically scanning where to best conceal himself. There was no true hiding spot. He ducked under the ledge next to the hole and prayed.

The splashing grew louder.

"What in Siria's skirt?! You said you tied him up!" Mett yelled, followed by the sound of splattering water.

Their footsteps were audible on what hopefully was the other side of the stream.

"I did!" Trauts bellowed back to Mett. "But I'm not worrying about that now. What are we going to do? How do we find Steff? All that blood—! She needs help."

"She's most likely dead," Mett snapped.

Dead? Heaviness sank in Alvie's chest. True, Steff was a poacher, but that didn't mean Alvie wanted her dead.

"But she . . . dead?"

"Aye, and we lost that baby turtle!" Mett said. "And now that fool has escaped with our eggs!"

"Who cares?" Trauts exclaimed. "We must continue searching for Steff! She might be . . . Either way we cannot merely leave her for the vultures, and what made her scream like that?"

Alvie gulped. What *had* made Steff scream like that?

Mett wasn't paying attention to Trauts. Alvie heard him rushing around their campsite, throwing items aside in his haste. "We need to hunt down that Alvie! He has the eggs!"

There was an echoing silence.

"Are you listening to yourself?" Trauts's voice was lowered. "I care naught for any of this anymore." Alvie strained to hear. "I'm leaving. I'm going to keep searching for Steff."

"Nay. You're not. You'll find that little field eel and retrieve those eggs! You still owe me. Besides, she isn't even one bit fond of you, Trauts!"

Trauts spoke in a voice so low that, though he tilted his head and strained his ears, Alvie couldn't make out what he said in reply.

"Trauts! Come back!" Mett's shout echoed off the rock walls. "Trauts!"

Splashing water filled the air again, and Alvie tensed his shoulders. Mett had crossed to the other side. Alvie's side.

Alvie sucked in a breath wondering if the pocketed knife would be a better choice than the spade he held.

"Where are you, you little vermin?" Mett's voice was close.

Stars.

The shuffle of Mett's footsteps paced overhead.

Then paused.

Then shuffled again.

Alvie waited for the moment when Mett's scruffy face would suddenly appear. 'Twas only a matter of time before Mett inspected over here. He tightened his grip on the spade, ready to swing.

"Mett!" Trauts called from a distance. "One of the spades is gone."

"Aye?" Mett's footsteps crossed back over the stream. "Think he backtracked up the mountain?"

Their voices grew distant and in moments, Alvie was alone.

"'Tis now or never," he said, throwing the rucksack over his shoulder. Slinking past the hole, he ducked under the overhang in hopes that the old streambed would lead him out.

CHAPTER
12

A lvie longed to speed down the streambed, but his pace could only be so quick with a sore leg, a battered body, and an empty stomach. He scanned over his shoulder every ten or twelve paces. The overhang above the path continued and though he hoped it shielded him, he was also extremely aware that the overhang grew shorter and shorter. In no time at all, Alvie found himself in a half-crawling position, dragging his peg leg and the spade behind him, inching down the streambed until he was slithering the last bit to the opening.

From there, Alvie hunched, rather than stood, surveying his surroundings in the bright sunlight trying to convince himself that he was not turned around. He was not lost.

This way? He'd walked a quarter-hour's time before realizing this was definitely not the way. This way led up.

That way? Not that way.

Finally, in a few hours, he came to the stream.

"Please be the right stream," Alvie whispered.

From above on the rock wall, he could have sworn he heard chattering. He dashed into the stream, his giant steps spraying cold water everywhere. Was this it? He wasn't sure. He struggled to think clearly. He could not concentrate, constantly distracted by the chill, or how the cold water made his stump sting, or the hunger twisting his insides and telling him he should eat the next stone lizard he spotted.

It was well after high sun that he reached the intersection of the two streams. Near the bank of the opposite stream, the scatter of stone lizard bones was visible.

"Stars almighty," Alvie whispered, catching his breath as he exited the stream. His balance felt off standing on solid ground without needing to brace against the rush of water.

Then he noticed the blood. Was it Steff's blood?

Stars, would Mett and Trauts be nearing here any moment?

Alvie hefted the rucksack, adjusting it on his back. The sindri turtle eggs certainly made it heavier to lug.

His gaze found the cliff some yards away.

Dripping water and leaving a trail of wet rock behind him, Alvie stepped to the edge of the cliff. He could just make out the fallen tree branches at the bottom.

He did have a rope in his rucksack.

And he *knew* where this path led. Gazing back at the stream, he considered. He could continue to follow it, but there was no telling where it led, how long it would take him to get there, and if it would eventually lead back to Goat—and his starstone club.

"Blimey." He ran his hand through his sweat-soaked hair.

Which way?

A boulder near the edge caught his eye. Alvie withdrew his rope from the rucksack, examining the eggs' condition as he did. He tied the rope to the rock. Checked the knot. Peered down. Checked the knot again.

And dropped the rope down the side of the cliff. It only reached half-way down the cliff's height, but as he surveyed it, he became certain that he could reach a tree branch from its end.

A predatory rumble of something unseen echoed up from the ravine at the bottom of the cliff. Alvie paused, half-wondering if he'd imagined it. He could not tarry.

"Nothing for it."

Chatter chatter.

The hoshefer was positioned on a rock on the opposite side of the stream. Had Alvie not been listening for any more odd sounds, he might have missed it over the current of the stream.

It spun, its bushy tail whirling around itself. Each time it spun, it paused with its ears perked, pointing its nose in the direction the stream led.

Alvie stood motionless, thinking.

He gazed in the direction that Mett and Trauts would come from. Seeing no sign of them, he turned, sober faced, back to the hoshefer and the unknown route downstream.

"All right. Let's go that way."

He untied the rope and let it plunge to the bottom.

"Don't want to make it easy for them." A small grin appeared on his face. It turned quickly to a grimace when the facial movements reminded him of his hurt jaw.

Alvie took a last breath and continued wading down the stream, the hoshefer leaping along the rock wall above.

IT WAS WELL INTO THE NIGHT. 'TWAS PRACTICALLY dawn. Alvie's teeth chattered as he waded through the frigid water, but still he kept stumbling down the stream. Then, to his amazement, he found himself before the pile of jagged rocks that had been piled to stop the stream. The water level had greatly decreased, either seeping through the tunnel or leaking through the rocks. Over this pile, down the twelve-foot cliff, and around the bend of the stream, he would find Goat waiting. Carefully, Alvie began to climb over what remained of the rock pile.

The hoshefer had disappeared hours ago. At first Alvie had wanted to search for it, but he'd thought better of it. With only a spade and Steff's knife to defend himself against Mett and the hulking Trauts, quickly exiting their vicinity and never encountering them again was a much better idea.

Alvie was atop the rock pile when he stopped for a breath. The first glints of dawn winked against the rock walls.

Just at that moment, further up the dry streambed trail, Mett and Trauts came into view. The two men came to an abrupt halt.

Blast.

"Give us our eggs!" Mett shouted. "And we'll leave you alive!"

"Not likely," Alvie shouted back and skated down the rock pile. He could make it. He could make it out of this!

"Ooph."

His peg leg was wedged in the rocks at the base of the pile. Beside him, the stream tumbled into the open air. Alvie discarded the spade next to him and yanked at his leg. "Come on!"

He was so close to Goat, his club, and escape.

"Come *on*!" Alvie shouted.

Trauts was on him. Alvie picked up the spade and swung it over his head, smacking Trauts backward to trip down the pile of rocks. He was back up before Alvie could free his leg. This time, the spade hit nothing but air.

Trauts snatched the spade and took a swing of his own. Alvie ducked in time, but just barely, the *whoosh* of it inches from his forehead. Alvie tugged at his peg leg, using his foot as leverage, while trying to wrest Steff's knife from his pocket. The knife sprang into his hand, but before he could consider what to do with it, the spade batted it out of Alvie's grip. It flew off the nearby cliff.

Trauts swung the spade, whacking Alvie's shoulder as he twisted to free his peg leg.

From the corner of his eye, Alvie saw Mett standing nearby, observing.

"Don't you grow tired of doing everything he says?" Alvie asked, getting in one lousy punch to Trauts's thigh.

"Get the eggs!" Mett yelled from the banks.

"Stop fighting this, I cannot waste time here!" Trauts shouted to Alvie.

"Then leave!" Alvie responded.

Trauts ceased swinging the spade and pulled at the rucksack, which was thankfully firmly strapped to Alvie's back. His tug forced the peg leg free, and Alvie, now loose, jerked backward, throwing Trauts off balance. Trauts fell with a splash into the water at the base of the rock pile.

Alvie stood and found himself staring down the cliff. 'Twas only a small cliff . . . of more than twice his height. That was still quite a drop.

Foothold. Foothold. Where is the foothold?

He spotted it and was over the side.

Careful.

Down one. Two. Three.

Pebbles dropped off the cliff and Alvie knew that Trauts stood there, gauging where the first foothold was.

"Jump!" Mett yelled in the background. "Get those eggs!"

Alvie dared a peek down. Then leapt into the pool of water.

Splash!

A noise from behind caught his attention. 'Twas not the hoshefer. Goat?

Alvie stood, wiping his face and trying to listen.

Splash!

Water doused Alvie from Trauts's jump. The big man lurched to his feet beside Alvie in the pool, towering over him. Trauts seized Alvie by his forearms.

"Enough. Give me the eggs!" His eyes rounded as he stared above them. "What the–" Trauts trailed off.

Alvie turned to glimpse the hoshefer standing on the cliff. Its bushy tail stood straight up, and it chattered fiercely. As fiercely as a mystical furry creature could, anyway.

Trauts's voice was hushed. "Is that—?"

"A hoshefer!" Mett had made it to the other side of the rock pile and stood motionless on the cliff, a few feet from the creature. "'Tis a hoshefer! It'll be worth all the gold we can count. Get it, Trauts!"

Trauts didn't move, but stood, still holding Alvie, gazing at it in amazement. Mett dove for it, landing precariously close to the edge as the hoshefer easily leapt away from his grasp and scaled the rock wall as if skipping up a flowering pine-oak.

"Mett! Careful!" Trauts shouted up, still distracted.

Alvie kicked Trauts in the groin. The man immediately dropped Alvie, hunching over in pain.

"Normally, I'd ne'er do that, but you know." Alvie vaulted the pool's edge, glancing up to make certain the hoshefer was still out of reach.

Above, Mett yelled to the hoshefer, "Come back!" The old man jumped again, reaching for the hoshefer. He landed right at the edge of the waterfall and toppled over the edge into the pool.

The sound was not entirely splashing. Some of it was too crunchy, a sound that could only be bones breaking.

Trauts moaned, reaching for Mett's body in the pool.

Alvie wouldn't wait around to see how this ended. He sloshed down the stream, the water blissfully low.

"Goat!" Alvie yelled as he rounded the corner.

The mule was gone. Stars.

Never mind that. Alvie had to escape. He picked up his legs and lurched toward the sagemary bushes near the opening of the gulch. Trauts's footsteps were right behind him.

Grrrowwwl.

Alvie halted. The sound was coming from the cave at the end of the stream.

Trauts ceased running, too.

Grrrowwwl.

From the cave stepped a stone lizard. But 'twas not the small stone lizards Alvie had encountered along the way. Or even a medium stone lizard. This stone lizard was as big as Alvie. From its long snout, many, many teeth showed. And stuck in its teeth was a rock necklace.

The lizard's long scaly tail swished back and forth.

Alvie retreated three steps.

Its beady eyes were fixed on him.

Alvie dashed toward the opening of the gulch, Trauts close behind.

The lizard moved with nigh impossible speed. Alvie was mere steps away from the opening, but the lizard was already there. It snapped its jaws at Alvie, blocking the way. Alvie changed direction and moved toward the opposite bank, but that way was useless. Where would he escape?

The lizard shifted its attention to Trauts. The big man took a swipe at the beast with his brawny fist, the only thing he could do.

The lizard prowled backward then leapt at Trauts, its tail swaying this way and that. Alvie glimpsed his opening and ran.

Trauts yelled, darting out of reach of the giant lizard's jaws, and swiped at it again.

Alvie was almost to the opening when the words registered.

"Help! Help me!"

Goddesses of the moon.

Without halting, Alvie switched direction, and desperately dove for the sagemary bushes closest to the cave. He exhaled, gently removing the rucksack from his back before clasping the starstone club in his hand.

He gripped his hero's weapon. "I'm comin', Trauts."

He sprinted to the lizard, who'd managed to sink its teeth into Trauts's shoulder. Blood seeped through the man's tunic, a crimson stain spreading at a horrifying pace.

Alvie smashed the starstone club into the lizard. It was hurled back an incredible three feet away from Trauts, who slumped against the rock wall.

"Did you eat my Goat?" Alvie shouted at the lizard.

He whacked the club into the beast again. The cracking of bone sounded. His empty stomach lurched at the sound and Alvie dry heaved. He regained himself and knocked at it again. A growl escaped the creature, but a groan followed. The swishing tail slowed. The lizard snapped its jaws again, but with less vigor.

Trauts moved off the rock wall and crossed the stream to the opening.

Alvie swung again but missed. The lizard snorted, its breath making Alvie's stomach churn again. He swung the club once more. This time, he didn't miss his mark. The lizard slammed into the rock wall, its tail still.

Alvie held the club over his head at the ready. But the lizard did not move.

Slowly, Alvie lowered the club. "Well, that's that, Trauts," Alvie said.

"That certainly was impressive."

Alvie stiffened. The voice was Mett's.

He pivoted. Trauts was nowhere to be seen. In the opening of the gulch stood Mett. He held his dagger. Alvie could scarcely behold him. Blood ran down his face from a gash on his head. His other arm hung twisted at his side.

"Stars, Mett. You look awful," Alvie said.

"Where did you put them?"

"Put what?"

"The eggs, you dolt!"

Alvie's gaze shot to where he'd left the rucksack. 'Twas gone.

"Stars, Trauts, I saved your life," Alvie muttered.

"Where did you put them?"

Alvie shrugged. "Ah, looks like your partner took them." He gestured to the opening of the gulch.

"You lied before. Where are they?"

Alvie crossed the stream, waving his club. "I don't have them! Trauts took them. Now, out of my way."

Mett swiped his dagger at Alvie with incredible deftness, considering his state. "I am not asking again!"

Growwwl.

Alvie gave the lizard a backward glance. Its tail swished again. "Come on, let's get out of here."

Alvie made to move past Mett, but the older man pointed his dagger at his chin. "Give me the eggs."

Abruptly, the lizard righted itself and lunged at the two.

"Move!" Alvie yelled, shoving Mett out of the way. The beast's jaws clamped onto air and Alvie swung the club. He missed and the lizard's claws caught flesh.

"Ahhh!" Alvie hollered, the pain from even this small gash on his shoulder surging through him. He stumbled, losing his grip on the club.

Mett staggered and began to teeter up the gulch, leaving Alvie.

Alvie reached for the club. The hot breath of the lizard was on him.

Chatter chatter.

The hoshefer was suddenly there. It stood on its hind legs. Stood *in between* Alvie and the lizard. It growled its own small growl. The hoshefer could fit inside the lizard's jaw.

"Get out of here!" Alvie grabbed the club, his knuckles white.

But before he could take a desperate swing, the hoshefer took a swipe of its own. Its claws ripped across the lizard's eye. The beast yowled as it careened side to side, its tail slashing. The hoshefer growled again. The lizard dove, its jaws snapping.

The hoshefer dodged the lizard, racing to the opening of the gulch. Racing toward Mett. The hoshefer skidded to a halt at Mett's feet, chattering and growling as the lizard pursued it half-blind.

Mett shrieked. 'Twas too late.

The lizard was on him; the hoshefer scurried away out of sight. The lizard chomped down, the sickening sound of tearing flesh and bone filling the air.

Alvie tightened his grip on the starstone club and sprinted up the gulch, past the lizard dragging Mett, ignoring the man's gurgling screams. He threw himself into an unsteady gallop, the peg leg's strap digging into his thigh with every step. He skidded around corners and past dizzying drop-offs, stumbled, overbalanced, and nearly slipped over the edge, but still he ran. His every breath burned, his wounded shoulder throbbed, his stump screamed: *stop, stop, stop*.

Alvie did not stop. He did not slow.

He ran and ran and ran.

Down the switchback tails, through the morning, even when he thought his lungs would explode.

CHAPTER
13

Racing down the steep and gravelly path, fearing for his life, did not distract Alvie totally. And as he arrived back at the bottom of the foothills, his shoulders slumped, and he dragged the starstone club at his side.

After all of that, in the end, he'd failed.

He'd come so close and yet, he would not earn his hero's title.

"What will I tell the Cibil?" he said, collapsing and eyeing his shoulder wound. He was fortunate the lizard had left him with only a gash.

As he'd hurried down the mountain, Alvie had followed a trail of blood that could only be Trauts's. Drops of blood led into the trees. Alvie had no desire to follow it. He gingerly touched his broken nose. Aye, he was fortunate.

Stars almighty, Alvie was parched. His eyes scanned the landscape in front of him, The Mort visible in the distance. He turned his head, not wanting to consider the sandy-dusty-lousy way back to Kage Duna. His stomach growled. Nothing but sagemary bushes.

He stood and wandered the area, gauging if there was *anything* else he could eat.

"Could go for those slimy mushrooms right about now," Alvie said to himself when scouting the eastern direction turned up naught but a pebble in his shoe.

After emptying the shoe and placing it back on his foot, he also adjusted his peg leg strap. To say his stump ached was an understatement. His amputated leg shook like a sapling in a storm with his every step on the peg leg.

He tried not to compare this day to other rotten days he had experienced. But being chased by murderous poachers, then a giant stone lizard, while being robbed by said murderous poachers, had to be near the top of the list.

"Fact o'matter is, today was rotten."

The afternoon sun mocked him.

He sighed. "And it ain't even over."

The western skyline was covered with a bit more foliage. Bushes and baby pine-oaks spotted the area. Everything was a bit greener. Which meant—

Chatter.

The hoshefer stood on its hind legs on a boulder, its tail merrily swaying back and forth. Alvie approached the hoshefer with caution, expecting it to dash off at any moment. But when he stood before it, the hoshefer hopped off the boulder and unhurriedly stalked to a cluster of pine-oaks.

Alvie followed.

"What the—" he gasped when the hoshefer came to a halt.

There in the dirt, sat Alvie's rucksack. He opened the flap and sure enough, six sindri turtle eggs were tucked inside. His brows crossed as he frowned into the distance.

Why would Trauts leave this here?

Chatter chatter. The hoshefer seized his attention. Next to a stick and a few drops of blood was the word 'sorry' drawn into the dirt. More drops of blood led into the trees.

Alvie slung the rucksack over his shoulders and grasped his starstone club, peering down at the weapon that had helped him defend Trauts.

A silver-toothed grin crossed his face. "Well, that's that, ain't it."

The hoshefer stood nearby, wrinkling its nose, and tilting its head to the side.

"You have somethin' to do with this? Never mind. I'm certain you did." He laughed and whooped. "Fact o'matter, you been followin' me the whole time. I know it. You threw that turtle shell down to me, didn't you?"

The hoshefer cocked its head in the opposite direction. It seemed pleased.

Alvie let his laugh ring out as he pulled a dried apple out of his rucksack. He popped it in his mouth and groaned in pleasure— leathery old fruit had never tasted so good—adjusted the rucksack on his back, then swung the starstone club to his side.

Nay, the day wasn't over after all.

"Won't the Cibil be chuffed when he sees this!"

Chatter chatter. The hoshefer hopped back to the boulder and onto a branch. It seemed to Alvie that it intended to be his companion on the trek back to Kage Duna.

Snap. A rustling in the trees nearby stopped Alvie mid-stride. He jerked his head back. Was it Trauts? Had he changed his mind?

"Come on," Alvie whispered, gripping the starstone club. He had already decided the day wasn't rotten any longer. He could not handle any more surprises.

He waited for whatever approached.

Then Goat trotted into sight through the trees.

"Goat! You didn't get eaten after all!" Alvie dashed to the mule and hugged it around its neck. The mule brayed indignantly.

"Ha! Wait 'til the Cibil hears this story!"

'TWAS UNDER THE SOFT PINK GLOW OF THE half-moon of the Rapture cycle that Alvie returned to the lake of Kage Duna. He'd been unable to completely skirt The Mort, and since he'd been forced to abandon his saddle and saddlebags in the bushes in the gulch, neither he nor Goat had much enjoyed Alvie riding bareback for more than the occasional hour-long stretch. But now the meandering path that Goat had followed found Alvie gazing out at the lake under the moonlight.

In the darkness, the sludge of Kage Duna that had been narrowly creeping into the lake upon his leave wasn't as visible, but Alvie observed that the lake *had* changed since last he saw it.

He dismounted Goat and turned to the hoshefer on its branch nearby. He couldn't help but wonder if he would have even had a chance of finding his way back here if not for the hoshefer.

"You've been a great help, lil' fella."

He felt a new presence nearby. The Cibil of the Nay Moon came out of the trees and joined Alvie.

Did he know I'd return tonight?

Alvie side-eyed the hoshefer's branch. It had disappeared.

"You've returned."

"Aye, you won't believe what happened!"

The Cibil gifted Alvie with a close-lipped smile. "Well, then. I better be seated for your tale. You're hungry, I'm certain. Come. I've made some supper for you."

In response, Alvie's stomach growled. He followed the Cibil toward the glade. The Cibil paused, removed something from his pocket, and handed it to Alvie.

"Leave this for your friend. He shall appreciate it."

"What is it?"

"Sowre root. Hoshefers love sowre root."

Alvie's eyes widened as he took the root and placed it on the ground near the branch the hoshefer had stood on.

"You may not see him again. Hoshefers are peculiar creatures."

Alvie frowned, scanning the area. If the Cibil said it, he was probably correct. "Well, thanks, lil' fella," he said, hoping the hoshefer could hear and understand him. "For everything."

Back in the glade, with Goat grazing on ground lilies with Kenn in the background, and over a meal of sowre root pie and roasted mushrooms, Alvie told the Cibil of his adventure, sparing no detail and making certain to give emphasis to particularly grand scenes of the tale. The Cibil did not exactly give the response that Alvie would have been accustomed to in relaying such a tale—no eyebrow lifts, no exclamations of awe—but he enjoyed the tale all the same. His half-smile proved it.

"And that's when I found my rucksack with these eggs." Alvie lifted one out of the rucksack and handed the warm sphere to the Cibil.

The Cibil nodded.

"I was thinking," Alvie paused for a remark, but none came. "About what you said. How the sindri turtles hatch in the Monas Territory, then trek here, and then trek back to the spot where they hatched later to lay new eggs. But what if the sindri turtles hatched here? Here in Kage Duna. What if they didn't need to trek all the way back to the Monas Territory because they hatch here and the only trek they had to make was to the banks of the lake?"

He felt his cheeks redden and turned quiet, waiting for the Cibil to quash this idea. But the Cibil said nothing and stroked his beard in thought.

"An interesting idea, Alvie."

Alvie's face brightened. "Aye? Fact o' matter, it might be worth a try?"

The Cibil's eyes twinkled. "It might be yet." He set the egg on his lap. "My thanks."

"I was right glad to help you, Master Cibil. And I want to say, you were wrong 'bout what you said before. 'Bout the world not requiring your existence and all. It does."

The Cibil nodded, not meeting Alvie's eyes, but instead focusing on the starstone club nearby.

"Speaking of existence. Be certain you keep that weapon close. Its journey is only beginning, you might say." His gaze seemed to pierce Alvie's soul. "As is yours. Be ready." The Cibil withdrew a folded and sealed piece of parchment from his pocket. "When you return to Dara Keep, give this to your friend. Tell him to not open it until the Mead Moon."

Alvie ignored the goosebumps prickling his arms. "Aye. All right."

The Cibil gave a satisfied nod and silence followed.

Alvie held his patience. He would not inquire about his hero's title.

Wait, he told himself. *The Cibil hasn't forgotten.*

But in the morning, as the two tramped around the edge of the lake to the opposite side, the Cibil had still not given Alvie a hero's title.

"This shall be a good place," the Cibil said, running his hand across the dry stalks of fallen weeds that lined the banks here. "This place gets plenty of sunlight and the long stems of the plants will give them warmth during the night."

Alvie built a nest for the eggs, the Cibil directing him on the specifications until the ancient man was satisfied. Then the eggs were placed together. Alvie felt certain they wouldn't be disturbed here.

"When will they hatch, do you think?" Alvie asked.

"Soon." The Cibil peered skyward before giving a curt nod.

On the walk back to the glade, Alvie let the Cibil's preference for silence win out and bit his tongue to keep from asking the Cibil if he could please give Alvie his hero's title.

Finally, the Cibil spoke. "I suppose you'll be on your way tomorrow morning."

"Aye. I reckon I should return to Dara Keep. You know, with the other knights."

This did naught to prod the Cibil. He remained silent.

Night brought nothing but a supper that mirrored the one from the night before and more silence from the Cibil.

As Alvie lay on his bedroll, gazing at the starry sky above, he couldn't help but feel disappointment nag at him. The Cibil had clearly forgotten about his hero's title.

Could he give himself one?

He decided he could, but it didn't sound all that great. *Good morrow, I'm Alvie the Splendid.* Nay. Defining his own hero's title did not sound splendid at all. What sort of hero named himself?

Mayhap the Cibil would be glad to be reminded of his promise to Alvie. But to ask again felt almost as wrong as simply giving himself a title.

It doesn't matter. You didn't save those lil' turtles for the title. You saved them because they needed saving and to help the Cibil.

Alvie had to repeat the sentiment in his head a few times before it became truly true. But after replaying everything that had occurred, down to the Cibil's half-smile, eventually it was true. He *had* saved the turtles because he wanted to help.

And 'twas with this last thought that Alvie grinned to himself and finally drifted to sleep.

In the morning, Alvie found a cracked old saddle and saddlebags in the Cibil's shed.

The Cibil waved him forward when he asked if he could take them. "I have no intention of leaving," he said with a flicker of a smile.

So Alvie saddled and packed up Goat and was ready. He'd slept much better than he had the first night and directly correlated that to letting go of this hero's title business.

"Well, I'll be off," Alvie said. He gave Kenn a pat. "Glad you're home now . . . friend." He didn't want to attempt the horse's real name again and certainly didn't want to say Kenn in front of the Cibil.

The Cibil led Goat over and handed Alvie the reins.

"Farewell, Alvie the August," he said.

Alvie's breath caught. A slow grin lit his face. "Did you say, Alvie the August? That my hero's title?"

"Well, it isn't your stable hand's title."

Alvie snickered.

"*August*." Alvie drew out the word slowly. "What does it mean?"

"It can be defined in many ways. Kingly. Regal. Majestic. Obviously, these terms do not fit you."

"Oh." Alvie's eyes found the ground.

The Cibil paused before resuming. "But 'respected' is another definition. Respect is earned. Not given or inherent like royal blood and a noble title with which one happens to be born. You've earned my respect, Alvie. As you clearly did with that man, Trauts, villain though he may have been. And from hearing your tales, 'tis clear that you have a talent for earning the respect of others who truly matter. And you will continue to earn respect, even as you set out on your next adventure."

Alvie's silver-tooth grin appeared. "Thank you, Master Cibil. I promise I'll do well by this title."

"I know you will. Farewell."

'TWAS A QUIET JOURNEY BACKTRACKING THROUGH KAGE DUNA. Little did Alvie whistle, sing, or tell Goat stories. He pondered the Cibil's words.

The hoshefer did not reappear. Alvie wished to see it once more, but knew that, true to the Cibil's words, it would not.

After several cold, wet days, he made it out of the swampland and back onto the main road that ran south to Dara Keep. Fortunately, the winter's snow had melted into early spring, making the return journey much better.

Before he knew it, he and Goat were riding up to the stronghold of the Order of Siria under a clear dusk sky.

"Who goes there?" the sentinel shouted down when Alvie had reached the gate.

"Hallo, Nevin!" Alvie shouted. He waved the starstone club above his head.

"Alvie? Is that you?" Nevin shouted back.

"Aye. 'Tis me. Alvie the August!"

THE END

ACKNOWLEDGEMENTS

Alvie is one of those characters who needed his own story. Alvie is, after all, someone who probably reminds us of someone we know. Someone who worms their way into our hearts and shows us the true meaning of strength in friendship. Alvie spent the first decades of his life overlooked, like some of the most remarkable people we encounter everyday. We just have to see them and let them teach us the true meaning of being a hero.

Writing a novel is hard. Writing this novella was harder. But Alvie has always been good company, and it was a pleasure to tell a tale in which Alvie could take the spotlight. That being said, I could not have done this alone.

For my readers, thank you for asking for more from me. An author is nothing without readers. You make me feel so "big time." Whether we chat at a bookstore, online, or simply unite through shared stories, we are connected. The world needs more people like you.

For the many booksellers, librarians, book influencers, and fellow authors who I now call my friends. Thank you for taking in the new girl! The book community is the best, best, best place to be.

For Lisa Gregg, my editor turned friend, this book would not exist without you. Your advice, encouragement, and humor made all this possible.

For Natalie Brianne, thank you for helping to make this book absolutely beautiful. You are amazingly talented, and I am so grateful.

For my mapmaker, Mayank Sharma, thank you for making Deogol a *real* place.

For my friends and family who grinned when I told them I was working on Alvie's story. Writing is a lonely affair, but your support, love, and cheerleading envelope me as I write.

For my parents, who've always told me I can do anything. And for my parents-in-law, who've always echoed that sentiment.

For my children, Sawyer and Annabel, you can do anything. You two are my heroes who I will always cheer on.

Last, but always first, for my husband. I love you "all the way to the stars."

ABOUT THE AUTHOR

C ambria Williams believes that storytelling is limitless, timeless, and transformative. Cambria is the award-winning author of *The Befallen*, Book 1 of The Unsung and the Wolf Duology. She writes fantasy fiction and contemporary young adult fiction that emphasize the magic of hope and the strength of love. Cambria loves traveling, reading, and taking walks with her husband. She has an MFA in Writing and lives in Utah. Visit Cambria online at cambriawilliams.com.

From award-winning author Cambria Williams

KEEPER OF THE WORD

Book 2 of The Unsung and the Wolf Duology

Famed knight, Sir Tolvar, the Wolf, redeemed and reborn, is finally home. Striving to establish his new life, he takes his rightful place as the Earl of Askella. But soon after, he's tasked by the sovereign to find the missing StarSeer, Elanna—gifted with the power to See the future in the stars—who has mysteriously fled her sacred city. Tolvar has the strange and irritating sense that new adventures are just beginning.

Yet once Elanna is found, she reveals that the Capella Realm's imminent doom approaches and they must act with haste. Tolvar swears to protect her. But the unknown forces they battle feel all too familiar. And still troubled by his past, and vexed with an itch for vengeance, Tolvar may not be as keen a knight as Elanna's quest requires. But if Tolvar cannot keep his word and safeguard Elanna as she strives to preserve the fortune of the realm, 'twill not only mean the extinction of the StarSeer's Light, but the shattering of an empire.